ELEANOR AMPLIFIED

AND THE
TROUBLE WITH
MIND CONTROL

ELEANOR AMPLIFIED

AND THE
TROUBLE WITH MIND CONTROL

JOHN SHEEHAN

RP | KIDS
PHILADELPHIA

Running Press Kids
Hachette Book Group
1290 Avenue of the Americas, New York, NY 10104
www.runningpress.com/rpkids
@RP_Kids

Printed in the United States of America

First Edition: September 2021

Published by Running Press Kids, an imprint of Perseus Books, LLC, a subsidiary of Hachette Book
Group, Inc. The Running Press Kids name and logo is a trademark of the Hachette Book Group.

The Hachette Speakers Bureau provides a wide range of authors for speaking events.
To find out more, go to www.hachettespeakersbureau.com or call (866) 376-6591.

This is a sentence inserted into the copyright page for the amusement of the author.
The previous sentence serves no purpose and contains no useful information. Please proceed.

The publisher is not responsible for websites (or their content) that are not owned by the publisher.

Cover and interior illustrations by Ira Khroniuk.
Print book cover and interior design by Marissa Raybuck.

Library of Congress Cataloging-in-Publication Data

Names: Sheehan, John, 1981– author.
Title: Eleanor Amplified and the trouble with mind control / John Sheehan.
Description: First edition. | [Philadelphia] : Running Press Kids, 2021.
Identifiers: LCCN 2020054157 | ISBN 9780762498833 (hardcover) | ISBN 9780762498840 (ebook)
Classification: LCC PZ7.1.S4995 Ele 2021 | DDC [Fic]—dc23
LC record available at https://lccn.loc.gov/2020054157

ISBNs: 978-0-7624-9883-3 (hardcover), 978-0-7624-9884-0 (ebook)

LSC-C

Printing 1, 2021

FOR DARLA, LYLA, AND ALICE

CONTENTS

CHAPTER 1

BRIGHTON UP YOUR DAY!

MIKU HAD ALREADY walked into a trap and she wasn't even a foot outside of homeroom.

"Hey, Miku, I like your dress," Constance said.

Danger, Miku thought. Her body tensed as she waited for the attack. She knew that Constance Jordan, one of the most popular girls in school, would never compliment her—this was a setup. If Miku said "thank you" or tried to engage, Constance would make even more fun of her. If Miku ignored her, then Constance and her friends would snicker and probably post about her on the chat boards. But if Miku answered back with sarcasm or a joke? Fought *fire* with *fire*? The consequences were too dire to even imagine. The safest choice was to stay silent and just absorb the mockery.

"So, you're not going to say anything?" Constance asked.

"She just gave you a compliment," Beverly added.

"That's so rude," Annabella said.

"I guess she didn't learn manners in her old school."

"But she says plenty in her dumb paper."

Miku kept walking as Constance and her two friends continued to harass her as she made her way down the hallway, simultaneously texting into their ZipTabs. The three tormentors were known as the ABCs and were eighth-grade royalty. Being a year younger, Miku was all the more defenseless against their abuse. Their jeers stung, but at least she'd gotten past them without causing too much of a scene. Her morning walk from homeroom to her first class was a grueling social gauntlet, and today she was off to a humiliating start.

Walking more briskly now, she glanced up at a hallway poster showing happy students in backpacks, huddled in a semicircle and laughing. A big yellow sun behind them was emblazoned with the words BRIGHTON UP YOUR DAY! in bold type. Miku snorted and kept walking. The poster reminded her of the Brighton Middle School that had existed when she first moved to town a little more than a year ago. It was a school that had welcomed her, where she'd made friends that she'd thought she'd have forever. But that place was gone now. It had changed with the new principal, his "special curriculum," and the election of the new class president.

The students back then had been different, too—dramatically so. Back then, kids had their different friend groups, and there were cliques, clubs, teams, and troupes. And, sure, there were the usual scuffles and grudges and drama, but at the end of the day, it had been *one school*. Now, the student body was bitterly divided, and not over anything real, so far as Miku could figure; it was all nonsense! The level of whispering, backstabbing, and gossiping that has been happening around school had grown out of control and was made all the worse by the blasted ZipTabs. Miku shook her head in frustration as she passed student after student with their faces scrunched up to their ZipTab screens, reading, believing, and reposting anything and everything they saw there.

The ZipTabs were one of the pillars of the new principal's "Technology-based Education and Socialization System." Every single student at Brighton was issued one. The new guy, Principal Marvin Peterson, had entranced the school board with his promises of "data-driven learning," "scientifically proven teaching techniques," and an "emphasis on STEM fundamentals!" And the best part: it wouldn't cost the school district a dime. Apparently, he'd found corporate sponsors to provide all the technology for *free.*

As if the smart tablet knew Miku was hating on it, her ZipTab began to buzz in her backpack, and she stopped for a moment to dig it out. The sleek aluminum machine was about the size of a small notepad, with the name "SuperInteliCom" etched in chrome on the back. It was more advanced than her smartphone and came preloaded with software and social media, custom made for Brighton Middle. Of course, all other technology was banned from school grounds. The notification on the screen showed a new group message from her friend Raji Chandrasekhar.

RAJI: Anyone up for TDCoPM tonight???

Miku chuckled. TDCoPM stood for *The Dragon Caves of Pfaylrimoth Mountain,* an old, obscure role-playing game that Raji had found in his uncle's basement. Raji, Miku, and their friend Tessa Wilkins began playing it as a joke, but now it had become something of a group ritual.

MIKU: Too much homework

TESSA: Can't. Going to a grindcore show.

RAJI: LAME:(What you two doing now?

MIKU: Um, walking to class

TESSA: Same. Passing the spooky library.

RAJI: oooOOooOoohhh . . . don't go in!!

TESSA: No way. I'm no hero.

MIKU: Please stop spreading anti-library propaganda

RAJI: Then you go in!

MIKU: It's closed! But also, no.

"Ouch!"

Miku had been walking while texting and inadvertently headbutted Mr. Funches, the lunchroom attendant, in the back.

"Oh! Sorry, Mr. Funches!" Miku said. "What're you doing?"

"Be careful, Miku!" Mr. Funches said. "And stand back, these machines are heavy."

Mr. Funches was guiding workers loading large, refrigerator-sized boxes into the cafeteria. The big cartons were labeled with wide, shiny stickers that read "SmartFüdz!" over pictures of leafy green salads, wraps, and smoothies.

"Are the lunches changing?" Miku asked.

"Yep. I actually just heard about it myself from Principal Peterson," Mr. Funches explained. "It's health food or something, I don't really know."

"What was wrong with your chicken patty sandwiches?"

"Ask Peterson!" said Mr. Funches, waving his hands in exasperation. "He wanted to bring in an outside lunch program. So, I guess say goodbye to my chicken patty sandwiches."

"Huh. Well, thanks, Mr. Funches."

Mr. Funches waved as Miku kept walking. She brought up her ZipTab and entered the name SmartFudz in the search bar, and a website popped up, along with more pictures of happy people and green, glossy vegetables. It read:

SmartFüdz! is food, the smart way! We take a data-driven, user-centric approach to nutrition that pairs a user's menu option to their optimized edible unit! Don't just eat food, eat SmartFüdz!

On its face, it looked like a lot of other buzzy, trendy health food websites, but it was missing a rather crucial element: information. There were no details as to what was so different about their food, what made it "smart," or what a "data-driven, user-centric approach to nutrition" actually meant. The only real information Miku could find was an address in the warehouse district of Union City. Miku was suspicious, so she texted her friends.

> **MIKU:** Have you heard of "SmartFudz"?
> We should investigate.

In addition to being Miku's closest (and only) friends, Tessa and Raji were also the other two reporters at *The Brighton Beacon*, the school newspaper. Miku had started the paper only a few months after starting at her new school. It was a scrappy operation, but they were tenacious. Miku had dived into the role of reporter headfirst and loved doing research and conducting interviews before settling in to write a thoughtful, engaging story. Tessa wrote fiery investigative pieces (her latest criticized the school district for underpaying the janitorial staff), while Raji penned the paper's humor column. They made a good team.

> **TESSA:** Never heard of it. Why?
> **RAJI:** SMART FUDGE!?!?!?
> **MIKU:** FUDZ. There's an umlaut. Anyway, it's Peterson's new lunch plan.
> **TESSA:** Ah, that's why you're all bothered . . .

MIKU: Of course

RAJI: I love fudge and omelets. Don't see what the big deal is here.

MR. OKAFOR: Shouldn't you three be in Social Studies?

Mr. Okafor was Miku's English teacher and the faculty advisor for *The Beacon*. He was also the journalism mentor to the group, and the one adult Miku considered a friend. She realized that they were texting on *The Beacon*'s group chat and quickly stuffed the ZipTab back in her pack and picked up her pace.

Miku crossed in front of the gymnasium, which was another painful reminder of the sheer scale of the school's transformation. It had been rebranded as The HyperBlast Super Battle Zone, a gaming arena outfitted for the virtual reality game *HyperBlast*. Miku had written a lengthy article criticizing the game, calling it "a cruel and pitiless exercise in wanton combat, with no educational merit or justification, whatsoever." Her piece was not well received, however, as the students of Brighton Middle loved playing *HyperBlast*, and Miku was widely ridiculed on the school's social media as a result.

Finally, Miku approached her classroom with about a minute to spare. She looked around the hallway for Raji and Tessa, since they were all in Ms. Brown's first-period Social Studies class. When she didn't see them, she figured that they might have beaten her, so she took a deep breath and headed toward the door. Normally, being in a class with her two best friends should be something to look forward to, but this particular first period also put her in very close contact with—

"Hi there, Newser."

The words caught Miku sharply in the back before she turned and saw Conrad Praeder.

"Conrad," Miku replied icily.

"Newser" was Conrad's nickname for Miku and her friends. Teachers might have thought that it was a friendly joke, affectionately referencing their shared love of journalism, but no. Conrad, and now much of the school, said the word in the same way one would say "loser" and take great care to add an exaggerated "ewww." Rather than give Conrad the satisfaction of knowing it got to her, Miku had decided to own the name.

"Let me get that for you," Conrad said, sidestepping Miku and opening the door to their classroom.

Miku said nothing, but she threw her shoulder into Conrad's chest as she passed.

Conrad chuckled as he followed her and headed for his desk. Miku tossed her backpack onto the back of her seat and quickly sat down as the bell rang. If Miku was generally ignored or loathed by everyone at school, Conrad was both loved and feared in equal measure. A star in the *HyperBlast* arena, Conrad was tall and handsome—to some, but definitely not Miku—and he always had a smirk that telegraphed his unending confidence. Despite being only in seventh grade, Conrad was popular among the entire student body and was even close friends with Annabella, Beverly, and Constance, which only raised his status to unheard-of levels. What bothered Miku the most, though, was that, against all odds, he swept the student council election and had been voted in as student body president earlier that school year, another first for a seventh grader.

Conrad had been relatively unknown before the election, and Miku suspected foul play—how else would he have been able to win?—but she had never been able to prove it. His position also allowed him special privileges, which were granted directly from Principal Peterson, on the school's social media feeds—and Conrad knew how to wield his power. The videos Conrad and the ABCs would post there were the stuff of legend and included everything from replays of *HyperBlast* victories to dance-offs, funny skits, to pseudo-confessionals, and all of them were devoured by the student body, making Conrad essentially a celebrity at Brighton. Students would mimic his floppy hairstyle, and his choice of sneakers would cause local shoe stores to sell out. And if Conrad "liked" something you posted on the boards, well, let's just say it was a *big* deal.

Of course, none of this mattered to Miku because, to her, Conrad Praeder was just an arrogant, conceited, vain, snarky—although she'd admit that he was occasionally funny—bully. She watched as her classmates tried to play it cool or catch his attention as he sauntered past to his desk, while Miku tried to summon psychic abilities to make him trip and fall flat on his face. Conrad slipped into the seat just diagonal from hers as their teacher started to take attendance. Miku sighed; it *never* worked.

"Settle down, folks, let's get started," Ms. Brown said, addressing the class.

Ms. Brown was an institution at Brighton Middle and had been teaching here since probably forever. She was a short woman with frizzled gray hair and thick black-rimmed glasses, and was known to take absolutely no guff. Her reputation was so legendary that even incoming sixth graders knew exactly who she was and all of the stories about her, like the time she assigned an entire class detention for passing notes; when she flunked Brighton's star wrestler out of a tournament; and worst, when she hid a student's disguised parents (both of them!) in the back of the class to watch their child misbehaving. Ms. Brown was blunt, eccentric, and irritable—and she was also one of Brighton's best teachers, according to Miku, and one of her favorites, next to Mr. Okafor, of course.

"We're beginning our unit on the Constitution today, and I know you're all excited. Should be, too, as far as I'm concerned . . ." Ms. Brown said before trailing off into a stream of mutterings, another of her famous eccentricities.

The class, in a now routine motion, reached into their book bags for their SuperInteliCom virtual reality helmets, which had replaced books in every classroom. Well, almost every classroom.

"Nah, nope, nope, noooope!" Ms. Brown called out, waving her arms. "None of that now! Who knows what's in the First Amendment?"

The class paused, helmets in hand, unsure how to proceed.

"Ms. Brown," Conrad said, "you know the VR helmets are mandatory, right?"

"Ohh! Praeder, sounds like you just *volunteered*," Ms. Brown shot back. "The First Amendment. What is it?"

"Because the new syllabus—" Conrad continued, unfazed.

"The syllabus is what I say it is, Mr. Praeder," Ms. Brown said firmly. "Understand?"

Conrad stiffened and started to say something, but Ms. Brown's fierce gaze must have made him think otherwise, because he simply huffed. A chill settled over the class, and from where she was sitting, Miku could see Conrad start to tap something into his ZipTab when Ms. Brown turned to start writing on the board. Miku raised her hand, an uneasy feeling building in her stomach, but Ms. Brown had turned back and focused on Conrad. It seemed like she would wait all day until he answered her.

"The First Amendment guarantees the right to free speech and freedom of the press!" Miku blurted out when the silence and the feeling in her stomach had grown to the point where she couldn't take it anymore.

"Thank you, Miss Tangeroa," Ms. Brown said after a moment, but her gaze never wavered from Conrad. "Close enough for my point. What that means is that the government doesn't have the right to control what people say. Because the truth shouldn't be silenced, don't you think, Praeder?"

Conrad smiled and said, "Of course."

"You see, history has shown," continued Ms. Brown, "that when powerful people try to control what normal people say and think, it often ends very badly."

Miku and the rest of the class glanced between Conrad and Ms. Brown. It felt like there was a very different conversation happening, something besides a history lesson, but Miku and the others weren't a part of it.

"How unfortunate that must be for some people," Conrad said, his smirk unchanged.

A moment later, the loudspeaker that hung in the corner of the room crackled to life. "Will Ms. Brown please report to the principal's office?"

The crackling ceased and an unnatural silence filled the room as everyone looked at each other with stunned expressions. It had to be a mistake. Never had a teacher been summoned to the principal's office; it defied the natural order of the universe.

"Ms. Brown, please report to the principal's office. *Immediately.*"

Ms. Brown glanced at the speaker, then back down, hanging her head for just a moment before she looked up and smiled at Conrad.

"In a rush to prove my point?" Ms. Brown asked.

"I don't know what you mean," Conrad replied.

"Class, I think this is goodbye," Ms. Brown said as she collected some papers at her desk and stuffed them into her canvas tote bag. "Do your homework and try to remember to think for yourselves, okay?"

"I believe we can continue our lesson in VR," Conrad said, turning to face his classmates as if Ms. Brown had already left. Silently, the other students began reaching into their bags again to retrieve their helmets and quietly put them on. Ms. Brown took one more look at her class, shook her head, and slung her bag over her shoulder as she tromped out of the classroom. The other students had already forgotten about Ms. Brown and were, apparently, now in the middle of the lesson about the Constitution, but Miku was too upset to simply put on her helmet and dismiss what had just happened. Without a word to anyone, she bolted from her desk and ran down the hallway after Ms. Brown.

"Ms. Brown, wait!"

"Miku! Get back to class," Ms. Brown said, not slowing down. "This doesn't concern you."

"But, Ms. Brown, why is this happening? Aren't you coming back?" Miku asked as she tried to keep pace beside her.

"I doubt it, but listen," Ms. Brown said. Then she stopped suddenly, taking Miku by the shoulders and looking her in the eye. "Be careful. I might not be up to date on all this techno-whosey-whatsee, or understand all these gadgets and doodads, but something is happening at this school. Whatever it is, Peterson thinks I'm a threat to it."

Miku's mind reeled, and she felt as if Earth's gravity had suddenly doubled.

"Don't get in his way, Miku," Ms. Brown said. "This is too big for you."

"Baloney!" Miku said, almost shouting. Then, catching herself, she whispered, "I don't care who's involved, I can't just ignore this!"

Ms. Brown huffed impatiently but looked down at Miku's reddening face and softened her voice. "All right, then, kiddo. Don't give up. But find some help, be smart, and be careful who you trust!"

"Okay."

"And one more thing," Ms. Brown said, leaning over to whisper into Miku's ear. "Sorry, can't eat, I've got to run."

Miku blinked and gave Ms. Brown a confused look. "What in the world are you talking about?"

"It's one of those things Principal Peterson always says. Remember it."

Ms. Brown patted Miku on the shoulder, straightened, and then continued to stride toward Principal Peterson's office, leaving Miku standing in the hallway with nothing but questions. To whom could she go to for help? She considered her parents briefly, but then dismissed the thought just as quickly. They had their own problems and probably wouldn't see just how monumental this moment was. Deep inside she had the feeling that Ms. Brown leaving was just the most recent domino to fall in the strange series of things befalling Brighton Middle.

She trusted Mr. Okafor, but he was one of the teachers, and she didn't want him to end up like Ms. Brown—and then it hit her. It was kind of a long shot, no doubt, but there was one person Miku knew could help. There was a famous reporter in Union City who always broke stories about criminal schemes, corruption, underworld fiends, and the occasional super-villain on her show. In fact, it was this same reporter who'd been Miku's inspiration for starting the school paper; she was sort of Miku's hero. Miku needed Eleanor Amplified.

CHAPTER 2

THE MESMEROSIN EXTRACTOR

ELEANOR'S BREATH WAS fogging up her binoculars. She grumbled as she wiped the lenses with her sleeve and peered again at the dark warehouse across the street.

"I'm starting to think that anonymous tip was a bust," Eleanor said to no one in particular. She had a habit of speaking her thoughts out loud. Maybe it was because of her job; after all, as a radio host and ace reporter, her voice was her most powerful tool.

Thunderstorms earlier in the afternoon had made for a chilly evening, but Eleanor's trusty raincoat was keeping her warm and dry. She'd picked it up on an adventure while tracking receding fjords in Stockholm some years ago. Or maybe it was Oslo.

Wherever it was, they'd known a thing or two about jackets, and this one was Eleanor's favorite for a stakeout. The only problem was that she'd spent all day watching this health food factory and hadn't seen any criminal activity. Or really *any* activity. No one going in or out, no deliveries, security guards, janitor—

Wait.

Something was moving in the southwest corner of the building.

Eleanor swept her binoculars back and trained her gaze on a darkened window. There it was again: a flashlight beam flickering around inside. And for a split second, she thought she caught a glimpse of two people. Or at least one person and something else that could've been a person or *possibly* a grizzly bear. But of course that sounded farfetched. Well, only one thing to do now, she thought as she deposited her binoculars into her coat pocket: check it out.

Eleanor approached the front of the warehouse with care and knocked on the heavy metal door three times. There was no answer. However, she thought she could make out a light scuffling behind the door.

"I can hear you in there!" Eleanor shouted, pounding on the door again.

Next to the door, an intercom buzzed to life.

"What?! Hello? Go away! Do you have a warrant!?" someone said. Their voice was gruff and didn't sound like someone who was having a very good night.

"Hello, my name is Eleanor Amplified. I'm a reporter and I've got some questions about the factory," Eleanor said into the intercom. "No, I don't have a warrant, but I could absolutely just call the police instead."

There was a short burst of electronic feedback from the intercom before it went silent. Then Eleanor heard a series of muffled thumps and clanks as the mysterious person behind the door fumbled with the lock. A moment later the door swung open, revealing a tall, gaunt man wearing a lab coat.

"So, um, you're a, ah, reporter?" the man said, trying to keep his cool. "What can I do for you at this time of night?"

Something about him was off, but she couldn't quite put her finger on what. What she did know, without a doubt, is that she didn't trust this guy. "This is the SmartFüdz factory, correct?" Eleanor said. "You work here?"

"Yes, that's right. I'm a, uh, lab technician," the man answered. He cleared his throat and straightened up a little. "Now is there something I can do for you?"

"I saw a flashlight through the window, thought it could be a break-in."

"A break-in? Oh, I don't think so, I didn't hear anything."

"And you're all alone here? Working?" Eleanor tried to shift a little to peek around him and into the dimly lit warehouse.

"Mmhmm!" he replied as he moved subtly to block her view. "Yep, just me, that's right!"

"Do you mind if I take a look around? Just to be safe?" Eleanor said in her most earnestly concerned voice. "Or we could call security?"

She pushed her hand into her pocket as if looking for her phone when the man blurted, "NO! I mean, *yes*. Go ahead and come on in!" He shuffled off to the side so that she could walk in.

"Thanks!" Eleanor said, striding in out of the rain. As she entered, she quickly brushed off the sleeves and hood of her raincoat, sending a spray of rainwater into the man's face. He sputtered and wiped his hands over his cheeks and mustache before giving her a pointed look. A sheepish smile had started to spread before— Hang on. That *mustache*.

It didn't look quite right on the man's face: it was too big, and the color didn't quite match his oily hair. Eleanor pretended to wipe her wet hands on her pants and made a mental note.

"I didn't catch your name, Mr. . . . ?" Eleanor said.

The question seemed to catch the man off guard, and an uncomfortable pause settled between them. He self-consciously ran his fingers over his mustache as he muttered a little to himself before he finally blurted out, "M-M-Midrovia." Then, shoving his pockets into his lab coat in an effort to stop his fidgeting, he continued, a little more confidently, "Gilmin Midrovia."

"Uh huh," Eleanor said as she unzipped her raincoat. Beneath it was slung her trusty tape recorder and microphone, Eleanor's two other most powerful tools. Both were well worn from use and travel, but they still worked, even if they were a little clunky.

"Mind if I start recording, Mr. Midrovia?" Eleanor asked.

"Recording? Why do you need to record this?"

"Just to be safe," Eleanor said with a shrug. "So is it okay?"

"Uh, yeah. Yes, sure, okay," Midrovia replied, less than enthused.

Eleanor nodded, and then she selected the red Record button on her tape recorder. "Now, how's about we look around this place, huh?"

"Sure, we'll start with the factory floor."

Eleanor followed the mysterious Gilmin Midrovia through a set of double doors, noting the security cameras and sensors along the way. Over the low thrumming of air vents, she could hear a commotion coming from behind the set of doors just ahead, but it didn't sound like machines or turbines or anything else mechanical. It sounded almost like a jungle. Or rather, it sounded alive.

"You make health food here, right, Midrovia?" Eleanor asked, now unsure of exactly *what* she was stepping into.

"Sort of," he replied.

Midrovia opened the doors and led her onto the factory floor. She looked around and could honestly say that it was not what she was expecting. Instead of industrial machines, ovens, conveyor belts, or vats of ingredients, there were plants. *Everywhere.* There were countless exotic, oversized, otherworldly plants lining the floors and climbing the walls like this was a greenhouse. Then, a few steps beyond the doors, near the middle of the room, sat a large cabbage. Actually, it was the largest cabbage Eleanor had ever seen. It seemed to be the size of a Galapagos tortoise—and it was *breathing.*

"Watch out for Cabbigula," Midrovia said nonchalantly, motioning toward the pulsing vegetable. "He can get a little grabby."

"*He* gets *grabby*?" Eleanor asked, her voice rising a bit.

"Oh, okay, so cabbages aren't a 'he' or a 'she,'" Midrovia reasoned. "It just feels weird to me calling Cabbigula 'it,' you know?"

"No, I meant, it can *grab me*?" Eleanor said, her voice rising higher as she backed away from the apparently dangerous leafy green vegetable.

"Only if you bother him!" Midrovia shot back defensively.

As she stepped backward, she felt something thick and ropy brush against her back and hair, so she whirled around defensively. Then she saw the bushy patch of vines, their tendrils snaking across the floor and up the walls to the ceiling where they dangled from lighting fixtures. Luckily, it just *felt* like they were trying to grab her instead of actually doing it.

"What exactly makes all this health food?" Eleanor asked, bewildered.

"We're not making food, exactly. It's more like ingredients. Additives."

"And that's healthy?"

"It's all made from plants, by plants! And also machines," Midrovia replied. "With a dash of fringe science!"

Eleanor continued to look around. She wasn't sure if any of this was real, but what she was sure of was that the words "fringe" and "science" shouldn't go together.

"What about this thing?" Eleanor asked, leaning over a globe-like device resembling a gumball dispenser that contained hundreds of little pink spheres. She gave the little lever a twist, expecting a gumball to pop out.

Instead, she got Midrovia shoving himself in front her, yelling, "Don't touch that!"

He quickly twisted the lever back to its starting point before turning and giving her a look. "That's a maltodextrose RNA recombinator! It could destroy this whole building!"

"Well, then it should be labeled, or have a sign, or *something*!" Eleanor yelled back. "And what does it have to do with health food!?"

"When used correctly," Midrovia explained, composing himself, "it makes a delightfully refreshing iced tea."

Midrovia continued the tour, pointing to the strange plant-machines and explaining the "nutritious" concoctions they produced as they made their way around the factory floor. One plant made a juice that tasted like chocolate milk, but with fifty times the protein! Another grew a fruit that looked like a cheeseburger, but tasted like a hot dog. "Still working out the bugs," Midrovia said with a shrug.

They walked past rows of various fauna, ficus, fir trees, cacti, and corn stalks. Lastly, they came to a round glass tank that was about the size of a microwave oven, containing a seaweedy, fungal mass. The light fixture above the moldy plant bathed it in an electric green light.

"And what's this smelly fella?" Eleanor asked, knocking on the glass with one hand and holding her nose with the other.

"This," Midrovia said proudly, "is the Mesmerosin Extractor."

"Great," Eleanor said, growing increasingly unimpressed. "What's it do?"

"Well, I can't really get into it," Midrovia murmured, stroking his chin. "The Mesmerosin Extractor is quite secret and very lucrative. But I can tell you this much: it extracts Mesmerosin."

Eleanor looked from the plant to Midrovia and back again. She'd just about had it with Midrovia's fringe-science nonsense and was about to say so, when suddenly a loud, staccato jazz number broke out from Eleanor's jacket pocket, interrupting the tour. It was Eleanor's mom calling. She had a knack for knowing exactly when Eleanor was too busy to take a call. However, Eleanor knew that not answering meant taking the risk that her mother was going to call back again and again and again, until eventually, if Eleanor continued to not answer, filing a missing person's report. So Eleanor answered.

"Excuse me a minute," Eleanor said to Midrovia, pulling out her phone. "Hi, Mom . . ."

Midrovia huffed and folded his arms.

"Mom, can I call you back, I'm in the middle of . . . What? Oh no, it sounds like you have to . . . Wait, back up, you filled out *what* online? . . . Mom, that sounds like a scam! How could you think a Tanzanian oil magnate would need help from you?!"

Midrovia chuckled.

"Okay, okay . . . slow down. I get it. It's confusing . . . No, that's understandable. I probably would've done the same thing. Don't feel bad."

Midrovia glanced over at the glass tank containing the Mesmerosin Extractor. The fungal mass was starting to bubble.

Midrovia coughed and raised his voice. "Ahem, excuse me! I don't have all night, madam!"

Eleanor glanced up and gave an apologetic gesture, pointed at her phone, and made a face that said *You know how it is*— even though Midrovia certainly did not share that sentiment. Midrovia looked back at the Extractor as it continued to bubble.

"Mom, hey, it's really no big deal. I'll make some calls and straighten it all out, okay? But I've got to go, I'm in the middle of an investigation and the subject is being extremely suspicious. All right. Love you, too. Bye." Eleanor ended the call, dropped the phone back into her pocket, and then raised her microphone back up. "Okay, let's continue!"

The fungus in the Mesmerosin Extractor calmed down; gave one last, gassy burble; and then stopped moving. Midrovia relaxed a little and, motioning toward the exit, said, "Well, I've shown you everything I do here. If there's nothing else, perhaps it's time to—"

"And the science? Your products are all tested and safe?" Eleanor asked.

"Yes, completely safe."

"And is SmartFüdz a private company? No stockholders?"

"Eh, yes, private. That's right."

"One last question, Mr. Midrovia," Eleanor said casually. "Have you heard of SuperInteliCom?"

Midrovia paused and his face dropped. Eleanor knew that her question had rocked his boat, but she was running out of time and needed to try to get some more information out of him.

"Ah, s-s-super who?" Midrovia stammered. "I don't know what you mean."

"I've been investigating a different company, called SuperInteliCom, for weeks. The problem is, I can't seem to find any information about it or anyone who actually works there."

"That's all very interesting, Ms. Amplified," Midrovia said as he fidgeted nervously and smoothed his mustache. "But what does that have to do with me?"

"I'll explain. Out of the blue, I got an anonymous tip that SmartFüdz is connected to SuperInteliCom. And that would make *you* the best lead I've got in this case."

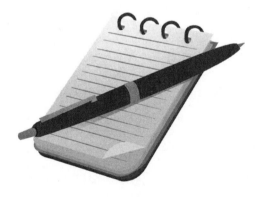

"But I don't know a thing about some mysterious technology company!" Midrovia exclaimed.

Eleanor cocked an eyebrow and took a step forward, her microphone extended toward Midrovia's face.

"Now, Mr. Midrovia," Eleanor began, "I never said it was a technology company."

Gilmin Midrovia paused and stared down at the microphone before him, which was capturing all of the caustic sounds of the factory floor. He avoided Eleanor's gaze, looking around as if summing up his chances of escaping.

"Look," Eleanor said, sensing his discomfort, "I'm just looking for information. I don't think you're doing anything wrong! I just get curious when powerful companies spring up and start throwing money around, but no one wants to talk about it."

"I suppose that's reasonable," Midrovia said cautiously.

"Sure it is," Eleanor said breezily. "So maybe you could show me some documents? Tax records, a business license, that sort of thing?"

Midrovia looked at Eleanor and once again at the microphone. Eleanor smiled back and wondered if her attempt at friendly persuasion was working on the shady lab technician. Finally, Midrovia conceded. "We keep the documents upstairs in the office, follow me."

Midrovia walked past Eleanor and up a flight of stairs to a metal catwalk that overlooked the factory floor and the strange, exotic machines below. He walked across to the far wall and then opened a door, showing Eleanor into a small office with a desk, computer, and a filing cabinet. *Not very impressive for what is supposed to be a cutting-edge operation,* Eleanor thought.

"It's all in the filing cabinet. Go ahead and see for yourself; we're a legitimate operation."

"Thanks," Eleanor said, but what she was thinking was that this seemed a little too easy. Usually criminals try to hide their dirty laundry, but she couldn't say no to being given free access to a trove of secret documents, so she dove in at once.

Sure enough, there were tax documents going back years, real estate deals and ledger sheets, invoices and payment receipts. This was exactly the kind of thing that would prove SmartFüdz was a clean, legal business. Except that the documents weren't for SmartFüdz. Eleanor snorted in frustration and flipped through more and more pages; none of them were for a company called SmartFüdz. In fact, they all seemed to be several years old and all made out to companies with a wide variety of different names. She looked up, expecting answers from Midrovia. But there was no one in the office with her— he was gone.

Eleanor dropped the papers and ran to the door and tried to turn the handle. Locked. A chill ran down her spine, and she cursed herself for letting her guard down. On the other side of the door, she could hear some sort of commotion, which was usually never a good sign. She looked around the room and tried to figure out what her options were. Her gaze stopped on the dirty window, but from this height, escaping that way wasn't really an option, so she braced herself, stepped back, and rammed her shoulder into the door.

It gave a little, so Eleanor slammed into it again, then twice more, until it finally gave way. As she stumbled out onto the metal catwalk, she could tell something was going haywire on the floor below. There was a loud sound like an off-balance washing machine that's overloaded with a soggy comforter . . . only bigger. Louder. *Squishier.*

Eleanor looked over the railing and saw the gumball dispenser, or the maltodextrose RNA recombinator— whatever—shaking violently. An explosion looked imminent. From her vantage point, she could see the whole of the factory floor. Unfortunately, the stairs to get down took her right by the blast zone, and she was way too high up to jump. On the far side of the factory, she saw shifty, no-good Gilmin Midrovia rushing toward the exit carrying the mysterious Mesmerosin

Extractor. From out of the shadows, a second man appeared—a huge, hulking man—who began to help Midrovia with the glass tank containing the Extractor.

"I see you, Midrovia, or whoever you are!" Eleanor yelled, her fist raised. "And I won't forget! This isn't over!"

Midrovia and the large man turned around.

"It certainly looks over for you, Eleanor Amplified!" he cried in a high-pitched maniacal voice. "I won't forget you, either! Come, Lars."

Then the two men ran out of the building, carrying the Mesmerosin Extractor between them, while Eleanor continued to run out of time. She scanned the room again, looked up, and saw it: one of the curling vines had wrapped around the light fixture and was just close enough for her to grab—if she leapt for it. The vine was long enough that she might be able to swing across the width of the factory. It was foolhardy, harebrained, laughably imprudent, and her only chance. Eleanor took a few steps back, then a deep breath, and then did a running leap from the catwalk. She stretched and felt her hand connect with the ropy vine, before her hands started slipping over its leaves. She gripped it tighter and she stopped sliding, and for a moment she was suspended, the vine holding her weight. Until it gave way, swinging her low over the ground floor.

Her hands slipped again and she let go of the vine, dropping abruptly into the waiting leaves of a horribly oversized cabbage. Immediately, Cabbigula's frilly leaves began to close in around her. Eleanor kicked and fought as the sound of the gumball dispenser grew more and more furious around her. With a final kick, Eleanor disgorged herself from the person-eating cabbage and launched herself at the exit doors a few feet away . . . just as the shaking, bubbling device exploded.

CHAPTER 3

ELEANOR, MEET MIKU

ELEANOR TOOK A breath and held it as the clock ticked down toward zero. Around her was darkness, except the glowing red light coming from the ceiling. She sat alone at a small table in the center of the room, inches away from a megaphone to the world.

There was a crackle as the studio's loudspeaker kicked on, and she heard the voice of her oldest friend, Barry Cunningham. "Eleanor, you're live in five seconds. Let's wrap this up."

Eleanor raised her hand and gave a thumbs-up. The red light on the ceiling turned green. Millions of people in cars, kitchens, basements, living rooms, bedrooms, and boardrooms waited to hear what she'd say next.

"We're back with *The Whole Story*. I'm your host, Eleanor Amplified. As regular listeners know, I've been investigating a powerful but mysterious technology company called SuperInteliCom. The corporation runs on dark money, and for weeks I haven't been able to track down a single employee, let alone information about its leadership. I'd hit a dead end.

"Then, out of nowhere, I got an anonymous tip that SuperInteliCom was possibly tied to SmartFüdz, a weird health food company. So last night, I checked it out. And listeners: that tip was right on the money, and it almost got me blown up . . ."

Eleanor recounted the story of the previous evening: the surreal factory, the exotic plants and machines, the Mesmerosin Extractor, and the strange man, a so-called Gilmin Midrovia, as well as his humongous, shadowy accomplice.

"I'm not letting go of this case," Eleanor continued, "and when I find out more, you'll hear about it here, on *The Whole Story*! I'm Eleanor Amplified. Until next time, listeners . . ."

The show's theme music played through Eleanor's headset as the green "ON AIR" light in the ceiling turned red again, and the room lights switched on. Eleanor's radio show, syndicated by radio stations around the world, was over.

Barry's voice came over the studio loudspeaker. "And we're clear. Great job, Eleanor!"

"Thanks, Barry," Eleanor said with a smile, removing her headphones. She stretched and rotated her shoulders, shaking off the adrenaline rush she got from doing live radio, and savoring this moment of calm before inevitably—

"Eleanor! Great show!" Eleanor's editor, Mr. Richman, burst into the studio like a typhoon. "Explosions? Shadowy villains? It's radio gold, Eleanor!"

"It didn't seem like *radio gold* last night, Chief," Eleanor said, rolling her eyes.

"Sure, sure, sure. Glad you're okay and all that, but come on, Eleanor! That's nothing out of the ordinary for you," Richman reminded her as he paced the small recording room.

Richman's nervous energy was the result of many years as a hard-nosed newsman. Given the choice, he'd always be on the move, sniffing out trouble, tracking down clues. But now, as the leader of a big news operation, he usually found himself pinned to his desk, taking phone calls. He *hated* phone calls. Anyway, Eleanor knew that his top concern was always for her safety, but sometimes his enthusiasm for a good story got the better of him. Eleanor was watching Mr. Richman pace when, a moment later, Barry, the producer of Eleanor's radio show, *The Whole Story*, entered the studio as well.

"That was quite a story, Eleanor. I can't believe this Gilmin Midrovia tried to kill you," Barry said, wringing his hands. "I mean, that's just awful!"

"Yes, thank you, Barry, for starting with the *correct* sentiment," Eleanor said, glaring at Mr. Richman.

"I said I was glad you're okay!" Richman retorted.

"Eventually!" Eleanor shot back.

"Look! Can we talk about what's really important here?" Richman said, pulling a newspaper from under his arm. "What are we going to do about this?" He slapped the paper down on the table. On the front page was a grainy photograph of the smoldering SmartFüdz factory.

"This just turned into a major case, Eleanor!" Richman said. "And why didn't you get anything on tape? Where was your recorder?"

"It was recording!" Eleanor said. "But it was destroyed in the explosion."

"Blast!" Richman said with a huff.

"Exactly," Eleanor said. "Anyway, this seems to be a major case, but I'm back where I started, with no leads."

As if in response, the red studio phone rang. The red studio phone was a direct line to Eleanor and rang only in *real* emergencies. Or when her lunch delivery had arrived. Or when her mom called. Sometimes, it was a wrong number. Well, *most* of the time it rang only for real emergencies.

"Aha! A new clue, right on schedule!" Mr. Richman boomed as he picked up the receiver. "Richman here, waddaya want!?"

Eleanor and Barry listened as Mr. Richman's responses grew increasingly more frazzled.

"A visitor from where? . . . Wait, she is the what, now? . . . And she wants to talk to Eleanor because . . . Well, she can't just barge into a . . . Whoa. Whoa! WHOA! . . . Okay, fine! Send her to my office!" Richman said before slamming down the phone.

"Boss," Barry said, "what was that about?"

"Well, it's a sign all right," Mr. Richman said. "But I'm not sure which kind. Eleanor, the source of your anonymous tip just showed up. Apparently, she doesn't want to stay so anonymous. She is in my office now, so let's go!"

Mr. Richman was already halfway out of the studio before Eleanor and Barry had fully heard him.

"Hey, what?" Eleanor called after him. "I don't like visi—oh, forget it, wait up!"

Eleanor and Barry hustled out of the studio and after Mr. Richman as he barreled through the crowded newsroom. Eleanor's colleagues, her fellow radio reporters, were frantically covering another news day in bustling Union City. The city hall reporter was bellowing into her phone, trying to pin down local politicians; the transit reporter was getting updates on a train stoppage that had snarled the West Side; and the arts reporter was playing back tape from an opera debut that had taken place that week.

Together the whole thing sounded like goats performing heavy metal, but despite it all Richman commanded his newsroom with ease. "Simons! Get over to city hall in person! Abdullah! Get verification from the director's office! Quah! Fix those levels! And this goes for *everyone*: I want recordings, people! Audio evidence! Proof! Get it on tape or it doesn't exist! And don't bother me for the next twenty minutes or you'll be covering the municipal dump!"

The room began bustling with a different frantic energy as Mr. Richman continued marching toward his office. Eleanor and Barry followed silently behind because they knew that when Mr. Richman was like this, it was better to simply stay quiet and do as you were told. They didn't want to end up at the dump, after all. A moment later, the three of them stood before a broad oak door with the words A. RICHMAN, MANAGING EDITOR stamped neatly in gold foil on it.

Beyond the door was Mr. Richman's musty, slightly cluttered office, which contained a wooden bookcase lined with books, a few framed pictures, and the occasional trophy; Richman's desk, which was strewn with papers and documents; and instead of a desktop computer, there sat five office phones arranged in a semicircle. In front of the desk sat two worn, leather chairs, and in one of those chairs sat Miku Tangeroa, waiting patiently.

Mr. Richman rounded his desk and sat in his chair while Eleanor and Barry stood silently by the door, evaluating the situation before them.

"Eleanor," Mr. Richman said, "meet Miku."

After a moment of puzzled silence, Eleanor replied, "Huh?"

Miku shot up out of the chair like a jack-in-the-box, her hand outstretched. "Hello, Eleanor, er, Ms. Amplified," Miku stammered, "it's so nice to meet you. I'm a really big fan. In fact, 'fan' sort of doesn't describe it, because you're like a hero to me, and—"

"Whoa!" Eleanor said, raising her hands in the international gesture for take-it-down-a-notch. "That's very nice of you, but what is going on right now? Who are you? How did you know SmartFüdz was up to no good? When were you born?"

Miku, hand still outstretched, responded, "My name is Miku Tangeroa, I'm twelve years old, and a reporter for my school paper. I've been investigating SuperInteliCom, just like you, Ms. Amplified."

Eleanor said nothing but began to rub her temples as she paced back and forth across the office. Barry closed the door, then slouched, stunned, into the vacant chair while Mr. Richman leaned forward on his elbows and watched his befuddled, so-called star-investigative team try to make sense of a middle school student beating them to a scoop. Eleanor was a *professional*. She had been solving cases, breaking stories, and bringing down the bad guys for years; this was sort of her deal. But right now, she realized that she was completely dependent on this middle schooler for information. Miku finally retracted her hand and sat back down as she tried to keep the amused smile off her lips while she listened to Eleanor try to figure everything out.

"Okay, Miku, was it?" Eleanor began, finally stopping her pacing. "Take it from the top."

"I'd be happy to," Miku said. "It all began at the beginning of the school year."

Miku opened her backpack and pulled out her reporter's notebook. Eleanor could see that Miku had been keeping meticulous notes, with dates, quotes, and sources. *This kid is serious*, Eleanor thought.

"Brighton Middle used to be a normal public school. Just like every other school I'd ever seen," Miku said. "But last fall we got a new principal, Mr. Peterson. He told us that we were behind the curve in science and technology. This was news to the school; our test scores were pretty good, and we had lots of science clubs—"

"Miku," Eleanor interrupted, "this doesn't sound that out of the ordinary."

"Are the big scoops always out in the open?" Miku countered.

"She's got you there, Eleanor," Barry said as Eleanor rolled her eyes. She was always impatient to get to the good parts—at least that is what Barry always said.

"Anyway," Miku continued, "Mr. Peterson introduced his plan for the school: a completely new curriculum with teaching and learning rooted in virtual reality."

"All right," Eleanor said. "Getting weirder."

"Principal Peterson said that every class had to be taught in VR, even gym class, which I'll get to in a minute, and he also brought in the ZipTabs," Miku said.

"That sounds kind of fun!" Mr. Richman chimed in.

"No," Miku said sternly. "The ZipTabs are the worst. They're super advanced tablets that are issued to every student, and they only operate on the school's network, no outside connections."

"Okay . . ." Eleanor, Barry, and Mr. Richman said together. They'd worked together for so long that sometimes their brains started to sync.

"We do our homework on the ZipTabs. They're our textbooks and notepads, they're how we communicate with our teachers," Miku continued. "But they're also how the students communicate with each other."

"Huh? How does that work?" asked Eleanor.

"I'll show you!" Miku said, reaching again into her backpack and pulling out her ZipTab. "Here are all my assignments due this week." Miku swiped her finger across the screen, dragging a workspace window into view with lists of worksheets, essays, and quizzes to be completed—although Miku had finished most of her assignments already.

"And here," Miku continued, swiping her finger in the other direction, "is the beating heart of Brighton Middle School's social life."

The screen shifted into an array of colorful tiles displaying message boards, flashing direct messages, and shared photos and videos. Across the top of the screen was a banner displaying recent bulletins: "1st Floor Boy's Bathroom Out of Order," "Click Here for Latest HyperBlast Scores," "Search for Social Studies Sub Continues." In one corner was Miku's school photo and below it was a list of all her connections and groups. In general, she tried to keep a low profile, but on the ZipTabs everyone was exposed.

"The ZipTabs are like every social media platform you've ever seen mashed into one, and the school controls it all," Miku said.

"What, like censorship?" Barry asked. "Because, I'm sorry to say, Miku, schools are allowed some control over a student's speech."

"He's right, Miku," Eleanor added, "that's legal."

"No!" Miku said, getting more animated. "They're manipulating us through the message boards! I'm sure of it!"

Eleanor, Barry, and Mr. Richman shared a skeptical glance, not even bothering to try to hide it from Miku. So she gave them a pointed look in return and cleared her throat.

"Okay, okay, listen, that's not everything," Miku said. "There's also the game, *HyperBlast*."

"Well, sure," Mr. Richman said, "the name alone implies an injury lawsuit waiting to happen."

"No, no," Miku explained. "It happens in virtual reality. Everyone has, like, these big dodgeball cannons and kids run around on alien worlds blasting each other."

"Whoa," Barry chimed in, an excited grin on his face. "Can anyone play?"

"Barry!" Eleanor chided. "Get your mind off video games for a minute. But, Miku, what's so dangerous if no one's getting hurt?"

"The kids are changing!" Miku said, nearly yelling. She gestured to her tablet. "The ZipTabs, the VR classes, *HyperBlast*—they're making Brighton Middle School *mean*. And SuperInteliCom is behind it."

That got Eleanor's attention.

"Okay, calm down, Miku," Eleanor said. "What do you know about SuperInteliCom's involvement with the school?"

"Well, the actual contracts and agreements between Brighton and the company are locked away—Principal Peterson won't give them to anybody," Miku said. "But I found a transcript of his presentation to the school board, and I found out that he said Brighton was getting *millions* of dollars in high-tech gear in exchange for helping the company conduct research."

Eleanor saw Mr. Richman's brow twitch, and Barry leaned forward in his chair, eager to hear what was next. She knew they could smell it, too—a ripe, juicy story waiting to be plucked.

"What *kind* of research?" Eleanor asked.

"He didn't say," Miku responded. "But he promised that all the technology would be free and that he'd get it through corporate sponsorships."

"We've been trying to find information about SuperInteliCom for months," Barry said to Eleanor. "There's no public information about the company anywhere."

"It's fishy," Eleanor, Barry, and Mr. Richman said together.

Miku gave them a funny look—the three of them were on the same wavelength again. Eleanor crossed her arms and thought back to the previous evening. The SmartFüdz factory had almost certainly been operating illegally, and someone was going to a lot of trouble to keep it quiet. But just like SuperInteliCom, it wasn't a fake or a shell; it was really operating and making things. So where was the money coming from?

After a beat or two of silence, Eleanor asked, "What about SmartFüdz? How'd you know I should check out that factory?"

"Well," said Miku, looking off to the side, "that was . . . a hunch."

There was a small pause as Eleanor stared at Miku, stunned.

"A hunch!? Ha!" Mr. Richman said, slapping his side, and breaking the silence.

"I nearly got *blown up* over that hunch, Miku!" Eleanor said, finding the comment much less funny than Mr. Richman had.

"I had no idea it'd be *dangerous*!" Miku said. "I saw these posters for SmartFüdz at school and heard that it was another of Peterson's ideas, so I figured they might be related and that it was worth investigating."

Mr. Richman was still chuckling as Barry and Eleanor shared a glance.

"After last night," Eleanor said, rubbing a hand over her face, "I'd say you were right."

"Look," Miku said, standing again, "I know I'm just a middle school kid, but something rotten is happening at my school, and this tech company, my principal, and my class president are all involved!"

"Wait," Eleanor said, holding up her hand to stop Miku while starting to rub her temple again with the other. "What does your class president have to do with any of this?"

"He's actually president of the whole student council and he's helping Mr. Peterson with his agenda!" Miku blurted out. "And I think his election was rigged! And he's a jerk, besides."

"Well, I don't know about all that, Miku," Eleanor began, then let out a sigh, "but something is happening, and your school is right in the middle of it."

Miku couldn't hide her excitement. "You mean . . ."

"Yes," Eleanor said with a glint in her eye. "I'm going to investigate."

CHAPTER 4

FIRST-DAY JITTERS

"HOW, EXACTLY?" MIKU asked as she and Eleanor approached the front of the school.

"The same way I start all my investigations . . . by jumping right in!" Eleanor replied with a smile.

Eleanor and Miku had agreed in Mr. Richman's office to meet the next morning in the school's front quad before school began. Eleanor studied her surroundings. Most of her investigations happened in slightly more exotic locations, like deadly jungles, seedy criminal lairs, or the lux offices of corrupt officials. This was the first time she would be in a middle school since she'd actually *gone* to middle school. She sighed. This was new territory for her, and although she didn't relish the idea of teaming up with a seventh grader, she needed a guide.

"But you're an adult," Miku said, interrupting Eleanor's thoughts. "You can't just nose around the school."

"Don't worry! I've got a plan."

Brighton Middle School was bigger than the other schools Miku had attended. Her parents' jobs moved her family around a lot, and Brighton was Miku's fourth school. The red brick building was topped with a white bell tower, and two marble columns supported an archway with the words DISCAT COGITARE, COGITARE VIVERE inscribed in the rock. It meant "Learn to Think, Think to Live" and had caught Miku's attention immediately when she first entered her new school. Beyond the building were the sports facilities: weedy baseball diamonds and soccer fields with long-faded goal lines, and cracked clay basketball courts missing the nets from their rims.

Throngs of students were converging on the campus grounds from the long line of cars and the nearby bus loop, filing in through the main double doors. As Eleanor and Miku approached, a distinct and loud electric hum could be heard over the bustle of students.

"What's all that racket?" Eleanor asked.

"Those are the new power transformers and cooling units—they're on the roof. The school uses *lots* of electricity."

"For what, a server farm?"

"You'll see," Miku said, nodding toward the entrance.

Miku and Eleanor entered through the double doors, and Miku quickly led her guest down a hallway and a side staircase, away from the crowd. At the bottom of the stairwell, Miku paused to give Eleanor directions.

"The administration offices are upstairs and down the hall from the lobby, but you'll probably want to avoid those."

"Where's the social studies classroom?" Eleanor asked.

"What? Which one?" Miku stammered, confused.

"Yours, I assume."

"Why do you need to know where my social studies classroom is?"

"Because that's where I'm going."

For a millisecond Miku was too stunned to say anything. Then, like a computer rebooting, the shock wore off and the words tumbled out of her mouth. "You can't go to class with me!" Miku said, straining to keep her voice at a whisper. "Have you lost your—"

"Miku Tangeroa!" came a man's voice from above them in the stairwell. The voice was authoritative, but not aggressive or barking. It actually sounded sort of pleasant, like a parent getting a sleepy child out of bed in the morning.

Principal Marvin Peterson descended the stairs and stopped at the bottom step and leaned against the banister. He was a middle-aged man of average height with thinning brown hair. His posture suggested he spent too much time behind a desk, or possibly hunched over a model train set. The only thing off-putting about the man was his choice of sweater vest, but only as an offense to fashion or tastefulness. He was, overall, nonthreatening.

"All this whisper-yelling, you sound like you're planning a bank robbery," Mr. Peterson said.

Miku straightened up, trying to be casual, but not too casual. She hoisted her backpack higher, and Eleanor pulled at her tweed blazer and adjusted her glasses—which were fake, obviously, but glasses are a necessity for any good disguise.

"Principal Peterson," Eleanor began, extending her hand.

Mr. Peterson regarded her for a moment, looked at Miku, and then slowly reached out his hand in return.

Sensing their budding investigation was seconds from being clipped, Miku panicked and blurted out, "She is my sister!!"

Eleanor and Mr. Peterson both froze mid-handshake. Miku held her breath, staring at the two adults as a bead of sweat formed on the nape of her neck.

"This is your . . . sister?" Mr. Peterson asked.

"Spiritual sister!" Eleanor said, slapping Mr. Peterson's arm with her free hand in a just-joshing-you kind of fashion. "We were just discussing our strong feelings about the freedom of the press."

Miku slapped her forehead but recovered quickly and pretended to be trying to swat at a fly.

"I'm a little confused," Mr. Peterson said slowly. "But your voice is mighty familiar . . ."

"The name's Eleanor," she said, taking her glasses off to polish them and buy herself a second to think. "Eleanor Agrandar. I'm the new social studies sub. We spoke last night," she finished, popping her glasses back on her nose.

"Ah! Of course," Mr. Peterson said, giving her an apologetic smile. "I knew you sounded familiar."

"Your student here—Miku was it?" Eleanor said as she motioned toward Miku. "She saw that I was lost and was giving me directions. I guess we got to chatting about the Constitution and, well, she's got very serious opinions!"

Miku froze as she processed this new information and was mindful not to let the surprise show on her face. Apparently, Eleanor had prepared more than she'd realized, but that's a professional for you. Eleanor glanced over at Miku and realized what was going on and gave her the quickest of winks. Not wanting Mr. Peterson to catch on and very much wanting to get him as far away as she could before he caught on to them, Miku tried to break up the meeting.

"Oh, I think I heard the bell," she said excitedly. "I can show Eleanor to her classroom!"

"No, no," Mr. Peterson said, "you'll be late for homeroom. I'll show *Ms. Agrandar* the way to her class."

"That's okay, Mr. Peterson, I'm sure you're busy—" Eleanor began.

"Yeah, I can take her, really!" Miku said just as the bell actually rang for the start of homeroom.

"Miku, your homeroom is on the other end of the building, and now you're late," Mr. Peterson said. "Get up there or you'll get a tardy slip. I'll take care of Ms. Agrandar."

Miku hesitated for a second, looking from Eleanor to Mr. Peterson. "Okay, well, see you in class Ele—, er, Ms. Agrandar," she said.

"Bye, Miku," Eleanor replied, keeping surprisingly calm despite now having lost her guide and being stuck in such proximity to the man Miku claimed was capable of nefarious crimes. Miku hiked up her backpack again and hurried away down the hall without another word.

Then Mr. Peterson turned to Eleanor. "Shall we?"

"Lead the way," Eleanor said with a wave of her hand.

As Mr. Peterson walked Eleanor up the stairs and down the hall to her classroom, he explained the school's approach to education and its emphasis on technology. Eleanor watched as his eyes lit up as he waxed about the positive effects of immersive VR and about the latest research in Copenhagen that "proved" students didn't need—or even want—intramural sports. It was all about the data, he explained; the reams and reams of data the school collected on student progress and behavior that could be formatted into useful spreadsheets. This guy *loved* spreadsheets.

"If you look at my spreadsheet of academic performance for this year versus last year under my predecessor," Peterson said giddily, "I'm talking about exponential growth, quarter over quarter!"

"Wow!" Eleanor said, reaching deep within herself to find an enthusiasm for quarterly reports. There was a reason that she didn't report on economic and business news.

"Wow, indeed," Mr. Peterson exclaimed. "Let me tell you, the school board loves me."

"And why wouldn't they, with results like those?"

"Right!? Okay, this is you," Mr. Peterson said, stopping at the door to the room previously used by Ms. Brown. Peterson opened the door, flipped on the lights, and led Eleanor in. The walls were covered in maps, posters, portraits of historical figures, and reproductions of the Magna Carta and Declaration of Independence, all of them layered like wallpaper, some looking like they were years, if not decades, old. Ms. Brown's desk sat in the corner, still cluttered with old exams and lesson plans. Mr. Peterson went over to the desk and, ignoring the mess, bent down and reached underneath it to pull out a glossy, colorful box.

"She really hated using this thing," Peterson said to himself, shaking his head. "Well, it's yours now!"

He handed Eleanor the box with a smile. On it was a picture of a shiny black virtual reality helmet and a pair of control gloves. The logo for SuperInteliCom was etched in the corner.

"Okay…" Eleanor said uncertainly as she turned the box over in her hands. It had some serious heft. "What do I do with it?"

"Put it on, silly!" Peterson said, turning to leave. "You already set up an avatar, right?"

"What's a Navatarite?"

"So, that's a no," Peterson said. "An avatar is your appearance in VR. It's fine, just put on the helmet and use Ms. Brown's avatar for now."

"That's it?" Eleanor asked. "What if I need help?"

"What did the gazelle say to the tiger?" Peterson replied.

Eleanor stared at Mr. Peterson. Then, after a beat, said, "Huh?"

"It's one of my favorite management riddles. Just think about it," Peterson said, "and good luck!"

With that, he walked out of the room and closed the door behind him. Eleanor looked at the box, sighed, and ripped it open. When she woke up that morning, she hadn't known she'd be teaching a bunch of tech-savvy tweens a made-up lesson in virtual reality, but here she was. She removed the helmet and gloves from the Styrofoam casing, put on the gloves first, and then fit the helmet onto her head. It was snug and a little heavy, sort of like a motorcycle helmet, and she couldn't see a thing. She began moving her head and hands and wondered if there was a switch or On button, when suddenly her entire visual field lit up.

A swarm of pixels swirled around her—at least, they appeared to—before crystalizing into a plain, blank room; the walls and floor were white and the ceiling glowed. Up and to her left, there was a small glowing sphere, about the size of a softball at arm's length, which stayed in her field of vision no matter where she turned her head. Eleanor looked around the room, and then held her hands up before her eyes. She almost gasped because her hands were now those of someone else entirely—and, from what she could tell, that someone was an elderly woman with a penchant for wool sweaters. This must have been the appearance of the previous social studies teacher, Ms. Brown. Then an automated voice sounded in Eleanor's headset.

"Welcome, Ms. Brown. Unread messages in inbox: two thousand two hundred thirty-two."

As the voice spoke, the words appeared in front of her, suspended in air, scrolling up and then dispersing into vapor as the
voice continued.

"Time to next class: thirteen minutes, fifty-five seconds."

"Current lesson plan: the United States Constitution."

"You're not Ms. Brown," said a real, nonautomated person-
voice behind her.

Eleanor spun around, hitting her knee on the edge of
Ms. Brown's real-world desk, causing her to grab her leg and
hop on one foot as she tried to breathe out the pain. As she
regained her balance—and composure—she looked up and saw

a man in her virtual space. He was strikingly tall and lanky, so much so that his slacks didn't even reach his ankles, nor the sleeves of his tweed blazer his wrists. He had an easy expression and friendly face, even in VR. He was also, Eleanor noted, rather handsome.

"No, but I'll be Ms. Black-and-Blue after this," Eleanor said, wincing from her bruised knee. "Now, can I help you?"

"Forgive me! I'm Adisa," said the man. "Adisa Okafor. I teach seventh-grade English."

"Oh, hello, Adisa," Eleanor replied. "I'm Eleanor, er, Ms. Agrandar. I'm the new sub."

"Okay, then," Mr. Okafor said with a laugh. "Would you like some help navigating the teaching VR? It can be overwhelming at first."

"Actually, yes, thank you," Eleanor said. "How did you know I was here or wherever I am?"

"I'll show you," Mr. Okafor said, gesturing to the space around her head. "Open your dashboard; it's that little ball in the corner."

Eleanor stepped forward as she swatted at the glowing orb, but it was just outside her reach. It was then that she realized that her avatar couldn't walk within VR, whereas in the real world she was walking—and bumping into things.

"Whoa, there; stop trying to walk!" Mr. Okafor said, laughing a little harder this time. "The motion controls are in the gloves; there are tiny buttons on your thumbs and forefingers."

Eleanor stopped and pinched her thumb and pointer finger together. Her avatar sprang to life and began moving around the blank room. After a minute or two she got the hang of it.

"Good," Mr. Okafor said. "Now point at the glowing ball and sort of poke at it."

Eleanor did as instructed, and this time the ball responded, opening a menu of information before her. She could see her class schedule, lesson plans, and student files. There was a pulsating icon in the shape of an envelope that indicated all of Ms. Brown's unread emails, a sidebar that showed all of the other teachers online, and a dropdown menu of locations: Principal's Office, Teachers' Lounge, Records Room, Library, etc.

"I saw Ms. Brown's icon light up, which was strange as she'd been let go, so I thought I'd come by and say hello," Mr. Okafor said. "Not that she ever used the VR anyway."

"I don't suppose I can change my avatar?" Eleanor asked.

"You'll have to take it up with Mr. Peterson," Mr. Okafor explained. "It takes special permissions. Except when you're in *HyperBlast*; then you can change into whatever you want!"

"Oh yeah, that's the game, right?"

"It's more like a religion for the kids here, but yes, that's right. You should try it out when you have a free minute. See what all the fuss is about."

"Sure," Eleanor said. "Maybe I'll check it out."

"If you like, I can help out, show you some of the gameplay?"

"Is it that complicated?"

"Not particularly, it just gives me an excuse to hang out with you," Mr. Okafor responded with a smile.

The comment caught Eleanor off guard, and she blushed furiously, although, thankfully, only in the real world. After taking a moment to compose herself, she chuckled. "You don't even know me! What if I'm a weirdo, or I can only talk about bowling, or I smell like anchovies?"

"I'll take my chances," Mr. Okafor said. "Well, see you around school, Eleanor. Bye!"

Then he vanished.

Eleanor took another second to think and realized that she had completely overlooked the counter in her dashboard that was ticking down to zero, and then the bell rang for first period to begin. She looked around her blank virtual environment, unsure what to do, before she removed her helmet and blinked as the harsh fluorescent lights hit her eyes. Sitting before her was a class full of seventh graders, waiting expectantly at their desks.

She saw Miku almost immediately, and she just stared back at Eleanor, jaw agape, with an expression that said, very loudly, "What did you just do?" Some of the kids looked amused with their hands over their mouths to muffle their giggles. A couple of them just looked plain embarrassed—for Eleanor, of course. And then there was the boy with floppy, dirty blond hair, wearing trendy sneakers and a malicious smirk, who had his head down and was typing furiously into his ZipTab.

CHAPTER 5

TO REFRESHMENT!

ELEANOR'S FIRST ATTEMPT at teaching wasn't a disaster so much as a slow-moving collision: nobody was harmed, but it was a spectacle and the damage was extensive. To be fair, any substitute teacher has a hard time commanding respect when coming into a new class. But when the sub carries on a personal— and sort of flirty—conversation with another teacher, oblivious to the presence of the entire class right in front of her . . . well, let's just say that respect was not earned. With the exception of Miku and the Newsers, Tessa and Raji, the class was completely out of Eleanor's control.

"Are you the sub, or did you get lost looking for a single's bar?" Conrad quipped.

Eleanor decided on leniency and let the comment slide. "Good morning, class!" Eleanor said, trying to regroup. "Sorry about that; this VR stuff is new for me."

"Is acting like a professional also new for you?" Conrad asked.

"Okay, twerp, show some respect!" Eleanor snapped, because leniency has limits. "You are a student, I'm the teacher. That makes you my junior. A subordinate. Below me. Subservient! Got it? Now pipe down!"

The class sat stunned for a moment. But, unfortunately, it didn't last long. Soon snickers and giggles began to break the silence like cracks in thin ice. Conrad sat cool as a snarky cucumber, his smirk a constant on his face. In Eleanor's world, arrogant and overconfident bad guys were pretty common, and she'd dealt with each of them in kind, but she had to admit, this kid had chutzpah.

Eleanor cleared her throat and began again. "Anyway, hello, yes, I am your sub, Ms. Agrandar," she said, writing her name on the blackboard, which caused another stir of giggles.

"What?" she asked, her frustration beginning to show.

"Ms. Agrandar," Miku offered, "the teachers here don't really use the blackboards anymore. We do everything in VR."

"Oh, yeah, right," Eleanor said.

"Ms. Brown didn't use the VR," Conrad said. "And look where it got her."

"What's your name, kid?" Eleanor asked.

"Conrad Praeder."

"Oh, you're Praeder. Popular kid. The class president?"

"That's right."

Eleanor paused. "Well, I've got my eye on you."

"I hope Mr. Okafor doesn't get jealous," Conrad said.

This, of course, earned him another round of giggles. Conrad glanced around like a lord holding court, making sure his subjects were following along. He might be an arrogant jerk, Eleanor thought, but his confidence was warranted. The other students were hanging on his every word. Eleanor knew she needed to move on or she'd never be able to get the class under control.

"Ms. Agrandar," Tessa said, raising her hand respectfully, "we were learning about the Constitution when Ms. Brown, er, left. The lesson plan is loaded in our VR helmets."

"Fine," Eleanor said, flustered. "Okay, yes, everyone take out your helmets and, uh, put them on."

The class did as instructed and Eleanor put hers on as well. Then she was back standing in her blank staging area, her VR dashboard showing the blinking lesson plan: "US History; Constitutional Convention, 1787." Eleanor selected the plan and a spinning ball of light appeared before her and under it the word "Loading..." After a moment the staging area dissolved and she and the class were standing in a slightly cramped, wood-floored statehouse that would become known as Independence Hall.

The class was centered in the assembly room, while many of the United States' founding fathers stood frozen in place: James Madison sat at his desk, taking copious notes; Ben Franklin slouched in a chair, fanning himself; Alexander Hamilton stood, arms crossed; and George Washington presided over them all in a stately manner. Eleanor could see the sweat on their brows from that swampy Philadelphia summer, though she couldn't feel it herself, and through the window she could see horses and citizens walking along the dirt street. It really was immersive.

"So, class, this is Alexander Hamilton," Eleanor began. "Does everyone know who he was?"

Another round of giggles came from the class.

"What is it now?" Eleanor asked impatiently.

"Nothing ... *Ms. Brown!*" shouted one of the students from the back row, prompting yet more giggles.

Eleanor looked down and remembered that she was using Ms. Brown's old avatar. *Great,* she thought, *one more thing to distract them.*

The class, meanwhile, all looked like themselves. Raji raised his hand and said, "Ms. Agrandar, usually we just run the simulation."

"Oh, sure, okay," Eleanor said, looking around for a big virtual Play button; then she remembered the dashboard. She looked up and saw the glowing ball in the corner, pointed at it, and expanded the menu. There she saw the lesson plan flashing and pointed at it.

All at once, the assembled founding fathers sprang to life, moving around the class, oblivious to their presence. James Madison began furiously scribbling, Ben Franklin continued to fan himself, Alexander Hamilton paced the room (arms still crossed), and George Washington listened to it all intently. It seemed like a decent enough historical reenactment, if not a little melodramatic.

"The chair recognizes the delegate from Virginia, Mr. James Madison," George Washington intoned.

James Madison stood solemnly, his wooden chair scuffing on the thick and worn floorboards. He took a breath and held it as he looked across the room of delegates, the bags under his eyes betraying his exhaustion and the weight of history he must have felt. He mopped his brow once with a lace kerchief and began, "Honored delegates, before I humbly beg of you to consider, once again, the import of a strong, centralized federal government, I want to give thanks to the most bodacious makers of SmartFizz energy drinks."

At that, James Madison produced a shiny aluminum can, holding it aloft for the whole general assembly to see, before cracking it open and taking a long, satisfying swig. George Washington ordered the sentiment added to the minutes as Ben Franklin clapped and then himself cracked open a cool, fizzy energy drink.

"We must cherish this freedom to choose and be refreshed!" James Madison began again, before Eleanor had finally had enough.

"Stop! Nope!" she said, jabbing at her virtual dashboard. "No more, stop, pause this thing!" Finally, she paused playback as the delegation raised their cans in a cheer, "To refreshment!" before freezing.

"This is not a history lesson, it's *an ad*!" Eleanor yelled.

The class stared back at her, their avatars expressionless, as Eleanor waved her hands around the simulation. And then, when they realized she was serious, everyone groaned.

"Um, no kidding," said Conrad.

"We tried complaining," Miku said, "but Principal Peterson didn't care."

"You can't watch anything for free without a few ads, right?" Conrad said.

"This is different!" Eleanor said, still gobsmacked that ads were popping up in supposedly educational content.

"Ms. Agrandar," Tessa said, "we covered it in *The Beacon* months ago. Everyone knows; no one cares."

"In fairness, we can all tell it's an ad," Raji added. "No one really thinks the founding fathers were swilling SmartFizz."

"That's the smartest thing you Newsers have said in months," Conrad snarked, lifting the tails on the waistcoat of nearby Gouverneur Morris, the right honorable gentleman from Pennsylvania.

"That's not the point, everybody," Eleanor said, before giving Conrad a pointed look. "This is our common history, it's the story of how our country started, and it's got to be something we all understand and see clearly!"

"Like how a bunch of rich, land-owning white men decided how it was going to be for everyone else?" Tessa said, matter-of-fact.

"Way to bring down the vibe, Tessa," Raji said. "Why not bring up their widespread oppression of women and people of color?"

"You should!" Eleanor exclaimed. "She should, we all should. It's fair game because it happened, and we all need to recognize it to make any sense out of what we should do for the future!"

Most of the kids in class rolled their eyes, but a couple didn't, and Eleanor took that as a sign that she was reaching some of them at least. "How the story gets told determines *everything*. It tells us who benefits, who loses out, who oppresses, and who are the heroes," she continued. "And if we let someone else tell the story, without questioning it, we're accepting their version of the world we live in."

"But sometimes things are the way they are," Conrad said with a cold stare.

Eleanor opened her mouth to give the little imperialist a piece of her mind, but she'd forgotten about the timer on the periphery of her vision ticking down to zero, again. Time ran out, the school bell rang, and the students instantly evaporated from Independence Hall. Conrad's face was still smirking as he disappeared, like an adolescent Cheshire Cat, while the Founding Fathers stood frozen in solemn dignity and collective celebration of an electrolyte-rich, sweetened sports drink. Eleanor sighed, bowed her head, and removed her VR helmet.

Back in the real world, in the time it had taken Eleanor to remove her helmet, most of the class had already evacuated the classroom. Miku, Tessa, and Raji remained, looking up at Eleanor with a mixture of sympathy and embarrassment.

"I don't know about jumping in, Eleanor," Miku said with a sigh, "but you definitely stepped in it."

"Ha ha, what do you mean, *student*?" Eleanor said, glancing at Tessa and Raji and back at Miku with a grimace. "Miku, was it?"

"It's okay, Eleanor," Miku said, nodding at Tessa and Raji. "They know everything."

"Yeah, you're Eleanor Amplified, ace reporter, master investigator," Raji said, bowing with mock reverence.

"Yup, that's me," Eleanor said dryly.

"But you make a lousy sub," Raji finished.

"Like you could do better, Raji?" Tessa teased. "She's not here to really teach us, she's going to help us bust Peterson and fix this school!"

"Tessa and Raji are the other reporters on *The Beacon*." Miku explained.

"We're basically the only normal people at this school," Tessa said with a shrug.

"Us and Mr. Okafor," Miku said, clarifying.

"You remember him," Raji said with a sly smile.

Eleanor rolled her eyes. "Yes, he was very helpful." She said, "He's the English teacher, right?"

"Yeah, and our faculty advisor for the paper," Miku said.

"He is down with the cause," Tessa said, folding her arms confidently.

"Definitely," Miku said. "I mean, he can't come out and say that he believes us, but he does!"

"Slow down, Miku," Eleanor said, sternly. "You guys are making some *big* assumptions and some *really big* accusations. And so far, by the way, I haven't seen anything out of the ordinary, except for some very questionable educational content."

"What?!" Miku said, throwing her arms in the air, motioning wildly. "You saw Conrad! You saw how the other students are around him!"

"He's a popular jerk, Miku. There's nothing weird about that," Eleanor said with a sigh as she set her VR helmet on Ms. Brown's desk, "I'm sorry. I'll keep digging, but I need *facts*, not conspiracy theories."

"In the meantime," Raji said, pointing to his watch, "do you think the rest of us can get to—"

"*Oh no,*" Miku and Tessa interrupted in unison.

"What?" asked Eleanor. "What class do you have next?"

"We're going to gym class. Now known as . . ." Miku answered before swallowing nervously, "*HyperBlast.*"

CHAPTER 6

NOW YOU'RE DEFENSELESS

MIKU, RAJI, AND Tessa hurried through the hall on their way to what was now known as the *HyperBlast* arena, before the bell rang for second period.

"So *that* was your world-famous reporter hero?" Raji asked, straining to keep up with Tessa and Miku. Raji was short for his age. He was short for any age, really, but it was especially noticeable next to Tessa, who was known in her family as "Beanpole." Tessa's natural stride often left Miku and Raji scrambling to keep up.

"I liked her," Tessa said. "It's not her fault. Subs have the worst job on the planet."

"Eleanor did fine!" Miku added. "Anyway, what is important is that she's on the case."

"I wish she could've come with us to *HyperBlast!*"

"Raji, don't be ridiculous. She's got classes to teach!" Tessa said, looking back to make sure Raji heard her.

"Yeah, we're going it alone. Like always," Miku said. "So what's our strategy this time?"

"Hide?" Raji suggested.

"It's never worked before. Why stop now?" Tessa said.

"I guess it's the best option," Miku said.

The gymnasium was a sight to behold. It had been pretty impressive when it was just a regular gym with polished wooden floors, but now it had been transformed into a spiderweb-like maze of wires, machines, and metal. Individual game pods were suspended from an expanse of aluminum scaffolding spread across the gym's length. The bars and cages hanging from the ceiling crowded out any natural light that might have squeezed in through the windows, so the game floor was illuminated by low-power LEDs, and because the machines and computer processors required lots of coolant, there was a fine mist that collected at their feet and added to the ghostly nature of the arena. From the loudspeakers overhead came the commands from Coach Tasker, the referee and gamemaster.

"Players, take your places! *HyperBlast* is about to begin!"

"Yes ma'am, Coach Tasker, ma'am!" Raji shouted, saluting the sky. "Looking forward to the humiliation!"

"Let's go, comedian," Tessa said, grabbing him by his sleeve. "There are three empty pods over here."

The pods weren't full enclosures but suspended body harnesses, with places to put one's hands and feet. Miku, Tessa, and Raji each stepped into a pod, folded the chest restraints across their torsos, and lowered the helmet units onto their heads. The helmet was substantially bigger than the VR helmet they'd just been wearing in class because it was built to accommodate the graphics necessary in the game. After a moment, Miku found herself transported into the familiar blank staging area, and around her she could see the other students' avatars, but they didn't look like themselves, like when they were in the simulated history lesson. Instead, they were every kind of creature and character imaginable: goblins, ninjas, Vikings, chimeras, a kangaroo, a leprechaun, several oversized eagles, elves, warrior-princesses, a few aliens, and many that defied any categorization.

Miku saw the glowing ball in the corner of her vision that would display the game's menu. She reached out, pointed, and jabbed at the orb, triggering the menu to materialize in front of her. She scrolled through her past avatars and settled on her most inconspicuous: a bush. The avatar that she selected pixelated and reformed into a leafy, green shrub that was about Miku's height. Within the staging area, her new bush avatar couldn't leave its spot, but it was able to spin and jump. She turned and saw Tessa- and Raji-sized bushes a few paces from her.

"What would Eleanor think if she saw us like this?" Miku said, mostly to herself.

"It's not cowardice if you know you're going to lose," Raji reasoned.

"I just hope the map includes a forest this time," Tessa said. "Otherwise, we won't exactly blend in. And the last thing I need today is to get caught in a BlastOff."

"Absolutely," Miku agreed.

As they waited for the game to begin, Miku and the Newsers studied the other avatars around them, but they were the only students who ever picked the bush avatars. Functionally speaking, none of the avatars were that different: they could all move in different directions, use the HyperBlaster, and pick things up or manipulate the game environment. However, some avatars were designed more for offense and others for defense. The bush avatars were the most defensive option. Most of the time, they were well camouflaged, and they could also duck quickly, pivot from side to side, or completely flatten to the ground, should the need arise.

Miku watched the blank space in front of her that would soon become the new map, the blue dots representing her teammates around her and her weapon selector, where she could see a slowly spinning bazooka-like object with a rubber dodgeball mounted to one end. This was the titular HyperBlaster that every player started off with. While other players were gearing up, wielding their HyperBlasters, Miku preferred to wait and keep her HyperBlaster hidden, to lower her profile.

To her right, Raji had scrolled through his game menu and selected the HyperBlaster, and it appeared nestled among his twigs. Raji pointed the blaster around the staging area, and Miku stifled a small giggle—it was funny seeing a bush aim a bazooka. Suddenly, he fired and the HyperBlaster ball rocketed off and hit a nearby troll avatar. The troll grunted, looked over at the Raji-bush, and then shook his head dismissively.

"Raji!" Tessa scolded. "You only get one shot! Now you're defenseless when the game starts!"

"I've still got my wits!" he shot back.

The HyperBlaster, or, rather, the HyperBall, was the only weapon that could eliminate another player from the game. However, the map allowed for other objects to be collected and used for things like trapping, immobilizing, or just generally smashing another player—but the ball had to *hit* another player in order to eliminate them. The HyperBlaster could only fire one ball at a time, but it was possible to reload using a loose ball or the ball of an opposing player. If one were desperate, or especially skilled, one could always throw their ball manually. Most game maps included caches of balls stashed around the terrain to give players a chance to reload. The object of the game was for one team to capture the other team's flag or knock all their players out of the game.

Coach Tasker materialized in the sky above them. She was imposing, with a muscled physique and closely cropped hair, wearing athletic shorts and a white polo shirt. A red whistle hung from a lanyard around her neck. Coach Tasker stood suspended in midair, one fist on her hip, the other clutching a bullhorn into which she barked, "Players, get ready!"

The staging area around them began to shift as the atmosphere swirled and a new virtual game world materialized before them. At first the terrain looked like the plains of the western United States: rolling grasses, a patch of forest nearby, and snow-capped mountains on the horizon. However, it quickly began taking on more alien characteristics as a stream of gelatinous green liquid oozed through the landscape, followed by a herd of supersized turkey creatures grazing nearby, and several alien moons visible in a purplish sky. And luckily for the trio, the foliage generally resembled Earth flora.

"Players, begin!" Coach Tasker yelled into her bullhorn before evaporating. And just like that, the game was on.

"Team! Gather 'round!" called out the troll that Raji had hit earlier.

The assembled team of avatars circled around as the troll started to give directions. As she listened, Miku recognized that the troll was her classmate, Michelle Collette, a gutsy seventh grader who, despite her bravery, excellent communication skills, and leadership abilities, still had not captured a single flag in *HyperBlast*. Michelle opened her map and began analyzing it with the others. They were currently positioned in a stretch of open field, their Blue Team's flag planted in the dirt a couple feet away, highly visible and approachable from many directions. This was a nearly impossible spot to defend, while the opposing team's red flag was located over a ridge, up a steep hill, and surrounded by rocks and uneven ground, which left them only one point of entry for an attack.

"Looks like we drew the short straw this time, gang!" Michelle announced.

"We always draw the short straw!" Tessa-bush responded. Miku knew that she would've rolled her eyes if her avatar had them.

The unfairness of the team's position was no accident: it was part of the game, and everyone knew it. The previous game's winners got to pick the next game's map, giving the winners a sizable advantage. And even though both teams were made up of seventh and eighth graders, the winning team happened to be mostly eighth graders and led by none other than

Conrad Praeder and the ABCs. In fact, they were so amazing at *HyperBlast,* they probably didn't even need the other players on their team in order to win. He and the ABCs were a terrifying force. They could somehow execute complicated battle campaigns and dispatch enemies with coordinated, but stylish attacks, and the replays were instant hits as soon as they were posted on the message boards.

Even their avatars were amazing.

Conrad's avatar was a version of himself as a winged Icarus, from the Greek myth, draped in a toga, but still wearing fashionable sneakers and sporting his trademark floppy haircut. Conrad's *HyperBlast* avatar was so iconic around Brighton Middle that some of the students even had T-shirts with it on the front, like he was the school mascot or something. Sometimes, after capturing an enemy flag, the four of them would form a pyramid, with Conrad on top, wings spread in triumph. Even though he couldn't actually fly—that would be silly—Miku had to admit that he did look pretty cool up there.

"Okay, Blue Team, not a lot of options here," Michelle said, attempting to rouse the troops and breaking Miku from her thoughts. "We'll need some defense and a lot of offense. Miku,

Raji, and Tessa, you three don't look battle-ready today. Why don't you stay here? The rest of us will blitz the Red Team's position and try to catch them by surprise. Okay, ready?"

"Um," Miku-bush murmured.

"I have some concerns," Raji-bush said, raising a twig.

However, Michelle and the others weren't listening. Her troll avatar raised her HyperBlaster into the air and bellowed, "Let's go!" before leading the rest of the Blue Team in a war cry of "YARRR!" And with that, the Blue Team stampeded toward the ridge and the enemy position, leaving Miku, Tessa, and Raji alone, standing by their flag.

"This isn't going to end well," Tessa said. "We should just run away now and hide in the forest."

"It *never* ends well," Raji said as he began trundling toward the trees with Tessa.

"Guys! Wait a minute," Miku said. "What if we actually *tried* this time?"

Tessa and Raji stopped and turned toward her.

"What's gotten into you?" Raji asked.

In the distance, they heard the battle yells of the Blue Team. The fight had begun. They couldn't make much out over the ridge, except for the dusty swirls over what had to be the field of battle. The intense cries of kids as they were hit with balls and others who cried in triumph lasted for about a minute, but then abruptly became silent. Eerily, even.

"I'm tired of running from Conrad," Miku said. "Let's stay and fight back for once!"

"Miku, you know that could mean—" Raji started, but then the Red Team's attack was already upon them. Seemingly out of nowhere, two dodgeballs careened off Raji and Tessa, knocking the bushes off their roots. Their avatars unceremoniously dissolved, forced to observe the final moments of the match from the waiting area. Three fearsome elf princesses—Annabella, Beverly, and Constance—charged toward Miku from different directions. They were clad in battle armor with designer shoes and expensive-looking yoga tights. Their serious style, however, did nothing to mask their ferocity. Moments later, Miku-bush had been disarmed of her HyperBlaster and pinned to the ground by Constance as a pair of fashion sneakers approached. Miku looked up and saw Conrad's smirking face, the ball of his HyperBlaster pointing down at her.

"I thought you usually hid during these battles, Miku?"

"I wanted to see what you were made of, Conrad," Miku replied.

"Challenge accepted," Conrad said with a smirk.

With a dramatic flourish, Conrad plucked the ball from the tip of his HyperBlaster and let it fall to the ground. Then he turned and faced his approaching teammates. "I declare a BlastOff with Miku!" Conrad yelled up into the sky. The game world froze as if, somewhere, a giant Pause button had been hit. Trees stopped swaying, birds hung suspended in flight—everything was still except for Miku and Conrad. She closed her eyes and cursed herself silently for walking into such an obvious trap. When two players were defenseless, one could declare a one-on-one battle with the other. A BlastOff put two players in direct competition in front of all the other players, who were gathered to watch. It was considered so potentially humiliating for the loser that there was an unspoken pact to never invoke it. And no one ever did, except Conrad of course.

When Miku opened her eyes, all the other players and Coach Tasker had materialized around the two of them in a large circle behind a force field. In the center of the circle stood Miku and Conrad, the only players who could interact with the game—including Coach Tasker—until the end of the BlastOff. The rules were simple: two players, two loose HyperBalls, no second chances. Only when one of the players was eliminated would gameplay resume.

The red rubber HyperBalls appeared in their hands—or, in Miku's case, her twigs as per the rules of the BlastOff. Conrad flared his wings, vamping for the crowd. Miku looked for Tessa and Raji in the crowd, and knew they were cringing in agony, even though she couldn't find their avatars. Then Coach Tasker barked "Begin!" into her bullhorn, and the BlastOff was on.

Conrad began stalking Miku from the circle's perimeter, forcing her to the center, while Miku kept her eyes trained on him, waiting for his first move. The assembled avatars cheered or booed, although Conrad was by far the most cheered—even by members of the Blue Team. His signature smirk was still plastered on his virtual face as he wound up, spun, and threw his HyperBall.

Miku watched the ball sailing toward her and at the last moment jumped to one side. The ball just missed, hit the ground behind her, and bounced up and off the wall of the force field. Conrad gaped for only a moment before recovering and scrambling to regain his HyperBall. Miku moved to the perimeter of the circle, giving her room to maneuver as she tried to force Conrad to the center this time.

"Nice throw, Conrad!" Miku yelled, trying to stuff as much sarcasm as possible into her words.

Conrad said nothing, but flapped his wings once in agitation, his smirk gone. Miku was surprised that she had managed to rattle him and hoped it would throw off his game. He jumped at her again, a little more recklessly this time, and again Miku was able to dodge his attack, this time by flattening herself to the ground. Conrad's ball sped by her and bounced off into another wall of the circle.

Tessa, Raji, and many more members of the Blue Team were cheering for her now from behind the force field.

"Keep it up, Miku!" Tessa yelled.

"Get him, Miku!" Raji chimed in. "You can do this!"

Miku allowed herself a brief moment of exhilaration, but knew she was still outmatched. It was only a matter of time until a ball finally hit her. Her avatar's attacks were painfully slow—because bushes can't throw balls very well—and Conrad knew that. Miku needed a plan and fast.

"There's only one way this ends, *Newser*," Conrad said.

"Does that mean you give up, Praeder?" Miku shot back.

"You can't win if you don't hit me! Take a shot!" Conrad said, but Miku knew that he was baiting her to throw, so that she'd be exposed.

And like that, a plan came to her.

"Fine!" Miku yelled.

She stretched back her throwing branch and hurled the ball with all her might at Conrad's feet. The ball left her leaves in a slow, light arc—something that every player could see was easily avoidable—but it gave her some time to square herself and prepare for Conrad's attack. He skipped lightly over the ball as it bounced and laughed as he once again wound up for a flashy, spectacular HyperBall throw. His wings unfurled as he kicked one designer-sneakered foot over the other, spinning his body to add to the ball's momentum.

The ball left Conrad's fingers speeding toward the very center of Miku's avatar. She held her breath, tensed, and spread out her branches as the ball connected, and then quickly wrapped herself around it as she fell to the ground. The ball was safely caught among her twigs and leaves. Miku laughed triumphantly; she looked up at Conrad as a look of anger and frustration spread across his face. The force field encasing the other students vanished, and Miku looked over at Raji and Tessa, who were shaking their leaves in excitement, hardly able to believe Miku had won. The game wasn't over, but she'd won a major symbolic victory: Conrad had never before been eliminated. The force field surrounding the players and Coach Tasker dissolved, the active players returned to their original positions, and the eliminated players—including Conrad—dissolved to watch from the waiting area.

But in that moment, as Miku stood victorious, a pulsating sound pierced the air.

Miku pressed her twig arms against her leafy head and looked around for the source of the awful sound. Coach Tasker stood a few paces away with her red whistle between her lips and a scowl on her face. The whistle gave another electronic shriek and seemed to distort the air around it, creating visible ripples in the game's reality. The other avatars near Miku, the ABCs, stood motionless and slack-jawed, staring at Tasker's pulsating whistle.

Miku watched as Coach Tasker stalked over to her and surveyed the scene angrily. She pointed at the ball in Miku's leaves, which vanished and reappeared on the ground. Then Conrad reappeared with a surprised look on his face. Tasker pointed at him, and then motioned to the blue flag, which was still hanging on its pole a few feet away. Conrad nodded, ran to it, and jumped up to snatch the flag. Coach Tasker gave another short burst from her whistle and spit it out angrily.

"Red Team wins!" she declared, raising her arms.

The ABCs were still dazed, but Conrad broke the silence with a cry of victory. The ABCs shook off their confusion and joined him for a celebratory pose as the remaining Red Team members rushed to their position and began celebrating. The floating scoreboard above registered the win, and a gong sounded, signaling the match was over.

"Wait a second—" Miku began, shaking her head. *Was this really happening?* she thought. *Had Coach Tasker just cheated and handed the match to Conrad and the Red Team?*

"You know you cheated, Conrad!" Miku shouted at the enemy avatars.

"What're you talking about, Newser?" Constance replied.

"Yeah, we saw everything," Beverly added. "Conrad won the BlastOff and captured the flag. Game over."

At that moment, Tessa and Raji reappeared at her side.

"We're sorry, Miku," Tessa said.

"Yeah, that was really close," Raji agreed.

"Wait," Miku said. "You guys, I beat Conrad!"

"Ha! Whatever, *Newser*," Conrad spat. "You'll never win against me. Now let's get out of here. I'm hungry." And with that, he and the ABCs vanished, along with most of the other avatars.

"It was the best showing by a Blue Team member that I've ever seen," Tessa said, trying to console her.

"No, no!" Miku said angrily. "Didn't you see me catch Conrad's ball?"

"Not exactly," Tessa said.

"We saw Conrad throw the ball," Raji said, "then you were on the ground, and the BlastOff was over."

"That's all I remember, too," Tessa said.

"I caught the ball," Miku said, almost in a whisper.

"Why don't we discuss this over lunch?" Raji asked, letting his stomach take the lead now that the excitement of the game had worn off.

Miku stared at the ball on the ground, which had started to evaporate along with the field and trees around her, just like the memory of her victory had somehow vanished from her friends' minds.

CHAPTER 7
SMARTFÜDZ, SCHMARTFÜDZ

ELEANOR'S NEXT SOCIAL studies class went a little better than the first; at least she'd managed to complete the lesson plan. However, she found it unusually difficult to get the students to take her seriously. Even for a substitute teacher, she'd had a hard time keeping their attention.

"Okay, everybody, good class," Eleanor said, removing her VR helmet. "Complete the homework listed in your ZipTabs, and I'll see you tomorrow!"

Some students mumbled an acknowledgment of Eleanor's presence, but most of them just packed away their VR helmets and left their desks.

"Questions, anyone?" Eleanor tried again. "Anything at all, okay? I'm available via text or email."

"You'll probably hear from Mr. Okafor," said one student in the back, which caused a flourish of snickers as the last students cleared out of the classroom.

"What was that?" demanded Eleanor, to more snickers. Then she groaned and turned back to her desk to start organizing her things.

"Kids these days . . . no respect!" said a friendly voice in the doorway, surprising her.

She spun around and saw Mr. Okafor leaning against the door, his arms crossed and a smirk on his face. He looked exactly like his avatar, or, rather, his avatar looked exactly like him: exceedingly tall with a kind face, wearing a tweed jacket and spectacles.

"Hello, Adisa," Eleanor said with a chuckle. "You've caused me some trouble today."

"Me?" he asked innocently. "What did I do?"

"Just ask any seventh grader."

"Why don't we discuss it over lunch?"

Eleanor coughed and turned as red as a turnip. "What? Um, today?"

"Right now! I'll show you the way to the cafeteria," Mr. Okafor said. "This is the only break you'll have to get some food. The same as me, coincidentally."

"Oh," Eleanor said, briefly considering the consequences of adding grist to the now buzzing rumor mill. "Sure. I could eat."

Mr. Okafor and Eleanor walked to the cafeteria, along the way chatting about the school: Principal Peterson ("He's really not so bad, as long as you like talking about data"); the students and cliques; and about Miku, the Newsers, and the school paper.

"The paper was all Miku's idea," Mr. Okafor explained. "She's got a very curious mind, but I think she was also looking for a way to fit in."

"Why's that?"

"Miku was new here. She'd moved around a lot, and I think she wanted to carve out a space for herself. She made some great friends in Tessa and Raji; they're peas in a pod. But nowadays I think the paper has isolated them. Ah! Speak of the devils..."

Eleanor saw the three students approaching from down the hall, also on their way to the cafeteria. Tessa and Raji looked concerned, and Miku had a sour look on her face.

"Hi, Miku," Eleanor called out. "Are you three all right?"

"Not really," Miku said angrily.

"She's upset because we lost *HyperBlast*," Raji said.

"Uh huh, well," Mr. Okafor started, "I know losses are tough, but—"

"I'm mad because Coach Tasker and Conrad cheated," Miku said sourly.

"Cheated by Conrad, huh?" Tessa teased.

"But no one seems to believe me," Miku grumbled as she lowered her head and skulked toward the cafeteria.

"I know what'll help," Mr. Okafor said cheerily, trying to change the subject. "Some *SmartFüdz!*"

"SmartFüdz, SchmartFüdz," Miku replied gruffly.

Hearing the name of the mysterious food company triggered Eleanor's memory of that night, days earlier: the bizarre factory, the plants, the sinister Gilmin Midrovia, and his hulking accomplice. That place in Eleanor's brain where her investigatory powers lived suddenly flared to life. Her nose twitched, her eyes squinted. Until that moment, Eleanor hadn't thought the school seemed that out of the ordinary—a little caught up in technology, sure, but not *threatening*. But on hearing that name, her suspicions were renewed.

"Let's see this cafeteria," she said.

Miku and her friends led the adults through the double swinging doors, and Eleanor could feel the three kids tense up on entering. The cafeteria was large and nicely furnished—much nicer than Eleanor remembered of middle school—with floor-to-ceiling windows that flooded the hall with light and colorful posters adorning the walls. Circular tables were arranged in groups throughout, and booths lined the walls, allowing six or so students to fit comfortably at each. Across the hall, Eleanor saw Conrad sitting at the center of a cluster of tables, surrounded by his acolytes. Miku, Tessa, and Raji quickly grabbed a booth on the far side of the room. Eleanor and Mr. Okafor followed, taking seats across from the students, whose faces dropped immediately.

"What?" asked Eleanor. "What's wrong?"

Raji, who was seated at the edge of the booth and so the most visible, slinked down in his seat, trying to hide. "Why did you sit here?" he hissed.

"They're embarrassed by us!" Mr. Okafor pretended to whisper to Eleanor, playfully enjoying the student's discomfort.

"Raji certainly is," Tessa explained. "He spends more time on the boards than me and Miku combined."

"Oh, your social media? The ZipTabs?" Eleanor asked.

The look on Miku's face said that she wasn't sure if Eleanor was playing it up like Mr. Okafor or if she really was that oblivious.

"Students are posting about us for just sitting here?"

"*Yes!*" Raji said through gritted teeth.

"No question about it," Tessa said.

"How can you tell?" Eleanor asked. She hadn't seen a single student so much as glance in their direction since they'd walked in. In fact, every student in the hall was looking in exactly *one* direction: down at their ZipTabs.

There was music being pumped in through speakers, but there was almost no conversation, save for the occasional chuckle, snicker, or exasperated gasp. The cacophonous din of every other cafeteria Eleanor had ever been in—even the small one at her newsroom—was absent. Kids sat hunched over their ZipTabs or huddled close together, sharing screens, all feverishly swiping and tapping out messages, comments, and memes.

"See for yourself," Miku said, holding up her ZipTab and turning it so Eleanor and Mr. Okafor could see.

Sure enough, starting at the top of the feed, Eleanor began scrolling through post after post of memes showing Eleanor making googly eyes at Mr. Okafor, or the two of them holding hands, or even, for goodness' sake, smooching. As she scrolled past the memes and snarky comments, what struck her most was the sophistication of the images. Students had already collected what looked to be dozens of photos of her and

Mr. Okafor and turned them into creative—albeit adolescent—memes. These kids had computer skills that rivaled those of her producer, Barry. One poster in particular, $Zra4Eva$, was especially impressive at photo manipulation.

"Am I in there, too?" Raji asked quietly, knowing the answer, but seeming slightly hopeful that maybe he was wrong.

"You know you are, Raji," Tessa said. "And it looks like Ziara got you good."

"Not *again*!" Raji groaned. "She's merciless."

Ziara "$Zra4Eva$" Ahmeed was known for her hilarious, although somewhat mean-spirited, posts. Last year, she was widely recognized as Brighton's top artist, having won talent shows and contests across the state. In fact, it was Ziara who designed the Brighton poster featuring happy students in front of the school. But now she was mostly just an online bully.

"She got us all, actually," Tessa said.

Eleanor saw that there was indeed a series of posts by $Zra4Eva$ featuring the Newsers: Raji at the water fountain, bent over awkwardly, with cartoon eyes drawn over his own; Miku with her arms crossed and horns growing out of her forehead; and a picture of Tessa cut off at her shoulders, with nothing but clouds above. She finished scrolling and handed the tablet back to Miku.

"Well, sure, they're well-made pictures," Eleanor said. "But they're not *clever*; I mean, as far as biting social commentary goes. I don't see why you're so upset."

"We keep telling you that, Raji!" Miku said. Even though, she had to admit, the jokes got under her skin, too, sometimes.

"Shh! Someone could hear you," Raji said, panicked.

"Okay, I can solve this," Mr. Okafor said, standing up. "I'm going to the lunch line; anyone else?"

"I'm in," Eleanor said, getting up as well, then looking at the Newsers. "Miku, Tessa, Raji?"

"I brought my lunch today," Tessa said, "and Miku never eats the school lunches."

"I have allergies," Miku said. "It's just easier staying away from food I don't know. But Raji loves SmartFüdz."

"I love all food, regardless of its intelligence," Raji replied. "But if you don't mind, I'll be going up there by myself."

Then he got up and bolted for the lunch line without looking back. Eleanor couldn't blame him, she supposed. He didn't want to add fodder to the ZipTab boards by being seen with teachers any more than he had to.

"The lunches are surprisingly good," Tessa said before taking her lunch out of her backpack. "It's the one thing Mr. Peterson's done right."

The two teachers looked at each other, and Mr. Okafor shrugged. "It is pretty great."

Intrigued, Eleanor figured that she needed to see what this *smart* food was all about. Then they left Tessa and Miku and headed for the lunch line, which already stretched around the edge of the room. As she waited, she shuffled back and forth a little, eager to check out the operation and see who was serving lunches. But to her dismay, as they approached the front of the line she could see that no one—that is, no *human*—was serving anything. In place of typical food stations or buffet lines, there were rows of gleaming metal kiosks, like futuristic vending machines, standing like sentinels. She watched as students stepped up to the kiosk, typed something into a touchscreen, and moments later out came their plates of food from a space underneath the screen. If she weren't sure SmartFüdz was up to no good, Eleanor would've been impressed. Up ahead, Raji had already gotten a plate stacked with what looked like chicken sandwiches and was walking back to the booth.

"You know, I heard that there was an explosion at the SmartFüdz factory," Eleanor said to Mr. Okafor casually. "How do you suppose there's still food here?"

"I don't know," Mr. Okafor replied. "I don't watch the news, but Peterson hasn't mentioned anything."

Eleanor looked at Adisa Okafor quizzically. It struck her as odd that an educator wouldn't watch the news or at least be aware of a somewhat major event in their city. But then again, she knew plenty of professors and scholars who'd rather have their nose in a book than pay attention to current events. Mr. Okafor was oblivious to Eleanor's glance and continued waiting patiently in line, humming to himself. The moment passed from her mind as her turn at the food kiosk came up.

"So, how do I work one of these things?" Eleanor asked Mr. Okafor as she stepped up to the kiosk window.

"Normally, it already knows what you want," he said, "but since you're new, it'll ask you some questions." He stepped up to his own kiosk and gave her a smile. "Nothing serious."

<<New User Detected>>
<<Please Enter>>
Your Name: . . .
Hair Color: . . .
Blood Type: . . .

Okay, Eleanor thought. *I'll play along for now.*

Your Name: **ELEANOR AGRANDAR**

Hair Color: **BROWN**

Blood Type: **A+**

<<Welcome, Eleanor Agrandar, to the SmartFüdz Experience.>>

<<Are there any substances to which you are allergic?>>

Answer: **NO**

<<Thank You.>>

<<Which item would you choose at a picnic:>>

A. Rice and Beans

B. Corn on the Cob

C. Caesar Salad

D. Grilled Asparagus

Answer: **B**

<<Thank You.>>

<<Which of the following best describes your dietary preferences:>>

A. Pescatarian

B. Paleo-Inspired

C. Ketogenic Mediterranean

D. Neo-Victorian

E. None of the Above

Answer: **E**

<<Thank You.>>

<<How would you describe your appetite?>>

A. I'll try anything.

B. I have a few favorites, but will avoid certain others.

C. I like one thing, and one thing alone.

Eleanor looked at her screen, feeling a little overwhelmed and very hungry. She glanced at Mr. Okafor, but he was already waiting for his food to be prepared. "Umm, I don't exactly know how to answer this."

"It's just lunch, Eleanor," Mr. Okafor said with a chuckle. "Don't overthink it."

Answer: **A**

<<Excellent.>>

<<In general, what are you most afraid of?>>

A. Spiders, Grizzly Bears, and Big Game Cats

B. A Listless Existence in the Void

C. Something Happening, Online or IRL,
   Without Your Knowledge

D. Societal Collapse

This is getting a little personal, Eleanor thought, *but I suppose it's harmless enough.*

Answer: **B**

<<Interesting. Are you sure?>>

Answer: **YES**

<<Fine, be that way.>>

<<On which of the following would you spend
the most money:>>

A. The World's Most Delicious Candy Bar

B. A Bland but Expensive-Looking
   Clothing Accessory

C. An App That Tells You Truthfully Who Likes You

D. A Time Machine

"What is up with this thing!?" Eleanor nearly yelled, growing more and more suspicious of this "health food" program's behavior. Though with such detailed questions, she wasn't sure how Miku wasn't able to find something that she could safely eat.

"I don't know about you, but I've already got my delicious tuna Niçoise salad," Mr. Okafor said with a delighted smile as he held up a plate brimming with strips of tuna and halves of hard-boiled eggs sitting on a bed of green beans and potatoes. "Did you know this salad originated in Nice, France?" he continued. "That's why it's pronounced *NEES-swas*. Now, traditionally it used anchovies, but I prefer—"

"Adisa, enough about your salad!" Eleanor interrupted. "This feels like . . . I don't know, like *data mining* or something!" Eleanor said, now uncertain if the strange feeling in her stomach was a hunch or just plain hunger.

"Mmhmm," Mr. Okafor said, apparently not hearing Eleanor, and taking a bite of tuna and savoring the flavor. "Cooked just how I like it!"

Eleanor hesitated for a moment, then turned back to the kiosk and finally selected:

Answer: **D**

This is ridiculous, there's no such thing as a time machine, she thought.

>>Final Question: Which best describes you?>>
A. I buy things based on what my friends like.
B. I shop frequently and like to show off my luxury purchases.
C. I buy necessities but secretly splurge on specific items.
D. I will buy anything advertised on a billboard.

For Pete's sake, Eleanor thought, but then reminded herself: *This is just so I can get a sample. I've got to get some physical evidence!*

Answer: **C**
>>Was that so hard?>>
>>On-Boarding Complete. Saving Preferences for Eleanor Agrandar. Your meal will be ready momentarily.>>

Then Eleanor crossed her arms and took a step back, her brow furrowed like when she did her taxes. But as promised, a moment later a little door below the touchscreen slid open, revealing a steaming bowl of tomato soup, one of Eleanor's all-time favorites.

"How did . . ." Eleanor trailed off, stunned at the machine's ability to serve up something exactly suited to her desire—even an unnamed one. And the *smell*! The creamy soup's scent wafted out from the chrome box, smelling of fresh tomatoes, basil, and garlic. It was nothing like the bulk canned soup she remembered from her school cafeteria: day-old, half-cold tomato puree in a Styrofoam saucer. *This* reminded her of her mother's tomato soup.

Eleanor removed the tray from the kiosk and the panel slid down behind it, resetting itself for the next student in line. She moved to the side, completely stunned, and put her tray down on a nearby table. She was hungry and the soup smelled irresistible, but she had a job to do. Eleanor quickly glanced around, then pulled a plastic container out of her satchel, and poured all of the soup in. As much as she wanted to try it, she knew that she needed to have it analyzed more, although she had a sinking feeling that it was what *she* had provided, not the kiosk, that would prove to be most dangerous.

That kiosk was built to do two things very effectively: dispense food and *gather information*. Information about the student population that could be lucrative for the right—or wrong—kind of company. Now, without a doubt, Eleanor fully believed Miku. There was definitely something criminal happening at Brighton Middle.

CHAPTER 8

THE TEACHERS' LOUNGE

BACK AT THEIR booth, Miku and Tessa finished their lunches—tofu lettuce wraps and a turkey sandwich, respectively—while Raji sat with his nose inches from his ZipTab.

"Any more zingers being posted about us?" Tessa asked in a monotone as she munched on her sandwich.

"Of course," Raji said with a sigh, "but they're getting less frequent. People have moved on to making predictions about the *HyperBlast* tournament."

"Yay," Tessa deadpanned. "Only a few weeks to go. I can hardly wait."

"I'm sure Conrad will win that, too," Miku said.

Tessa and Raji nodded their sullen agreement. Miku stared down at the scraps of her boring lettuce wrap. She didn't get a lot of variety with her lunches, due to her food allergies. In fact, her allergies had been yet another reason it was difficult for her to fit in at Brighton. For one thing, she hadn't spent years in elementary school with the other students. For another, her mom's job—she was a military surgeon—meant that in addition to the family moving around a lot, her mom couldn't be part of the usual school activities; she didn't chaperone field trips, or volunteer at bake sales, or go to PTO meetings. And Miku's dad was too busy managing the household and worrying about his own job to participate. Those things weren't important to Miku, but she noticed that the students with families who did engage in things like that tended to know more people. And have more friends. Miku only had Tessa and Raji now.

"I've been thinking. I know Conrad is popular—" Miku began.

"Thinking about Conrad?" Tessa interrupted. "There's a surprise."

Miku ignored her and continued. "He's popular, but how do all his posts get so much attention? Like, everything! It could be him eating cereal, and *boom*: top of my feed."

"You know, it's, like, the algorithm or something," Raji said. "The more popular he is, the more people see and click his posts, then the more popular he gets, and on and on."

"It's a vicious cycle. Or, should I say, *vacuous* cycle," Tessa said with a smile, waiting to see if her friends would get the joke.

"But everything?" Miku said, growing agitated. "And who made this *algorithm*?"

Tessa waited a beat more, and then finished up the last bite of her sandwich.

Raji shrugged. "But you know what's weird? He hasn't posted anything from today's *HyperBlast* match."

"So?" Tessa replied.

"Ha!" Miku said excitedly. "You see? He always posts something from the game. This is a cover-up!"

"Whoa, Miku," Tessa said, giving her friend a look. "You know that doesn't prove a thing."

Eleanor returned to the booth, waving goodbye to Mr. Okafor, who was leaving to prepare for his next class.

Tessa looked at Eleanor's empty hands. "I thought you were getting a school lunch?"

"I did," Eleanor said, sitting down and patting her satchel.

Tessa gave Eleanor's bag a confused glance, but the others didn't seem to mind.

"Listen," Eleanor said, leaning over and lowering her voice, "I've got to sneak off school grounds next period. I don't have class, but cover for me if anyone asks, okay?"

"Sure," Raji said with a shrug, his eyes never once leaving his ZipTab.

"What're you going to do?" Miku asked, trying to squeeze a little more information out of this new development. And hoping, just a bit, that maybe Eleanor would bring her along on this much more interesting and adult investigation.

"I'm getting this lunch analyzed," Eleanor said in a hushed whisper. "I need to know how it was made. That computer-kiosk thing knew exactly what I wanted!"

"Algorithms," Raji said with another shrug.

Eleanor glanced over her shoulder and around the cafeteria uneasily. She'd investigated too many shady companies to not recognize a serious violation of privacy when she saw one. And at a public school, no less! This case could be a whopper, and she needed to start gathering documentation as soon as possible.

"I'll be back, but I've got to get this soup to my producer," Eleanor said, getting up to leave.

"Eleanor, wait," Miku said, as a plan started forming. "Can I use your classroom to study while you're gone? I've got study hall, but, ah, they closed the library and—"

"Sure, fine, just don't get caught, okay?" Eleanor said, only half-listening as she slung her satchel back over her shoulder. "See you guys soon."

Raji and Tessa stared at Miku as Eleanor left, but didn't say anything. They could tell when Miku was up to something, and it seemed like she was *really* up to something now. It was true, the library had closed after the school began using the ZipTabs—no more need for books, after all—but they always used *The Beacon* office to study: it was their headquarters, a second home, and their fortress against the forces of darkness. There was no reason that either of them could think of that would explain why Miku would want to study in a classroom.

"I don't want to study in that classroom," Miku said, leaning down conspiratorially once she knew Eleanor wasn't coming back.

"No kidding," Raji and Tessa replied, both intrigued by the sudden mysteriousness of the situation.

"Meet me in Ms. Brown's classroom in a few minutes," Miku whispered. "Split up, don't draw attention to yourself, and take different routes to get there."

"Are you first going to tell us what you're up to, Miku?" Tessa asked.

"I'm jumping right in!" she exclaimed with a huge grin on her face.

....

Miku slipped through the door to Ms. Brown's former classroom and pulled the shade down over the window. She pressed her back to the door and shut her eyes. What she had in mind was dangerous; if she was caught, she'd be suspended for sure. Maybe even expelled. And how her parents would love that. However, Miku took a deep breath and stifled those thoughts because she'd come too far to stop now. A moment later there was a light knock at the door. Miku cracked it, saw Tessa, and gestured her inside. The two silently waited for the sound of foot traffic outside to quiet as students made their way to their fourth-period classes. A moment later, Raji arrived.

"So what are we—" he said, making the other two jump slightly.

"Shh," Miku hushed, a finger over her lips. "I'm going to use Ms. Brown's headset to sneak around the high-security VR."

Tessa and Raji stared at her, dumbfounded.

"Miku, this is the worst—" Tessa started.

"I'm in!" Raji said before quickly making his way to Ms. Brown's desk to pull out the heavier, teacher-sized headset.

"You two, stop!" Tessa said in an urgent whisper. "This is no joke. If we're caught, it's suspension. *For all of us.*"

"Tessa, I know," Miku said, "and if you want to leave, I'll understand. We're breaking the rules, and I have to do this, but you don't."

Tessa considered a moment and folded her arms. "I'll stay. Just hurry!"

"What're you gonna do in there?" Raji whispered excitedly.

"I need evidence," Miku said, taking the helmet from Raji and looking it over. "And teachers have advanced privileges in VR, so I might be able to learn something. Wish me luck!" And then, without waiting for their response, Miku plunked the helmet onto her head and fired up the VR staging environment.

Tessa and Raji exchanged nervous glances and took up their watch positions.

Suddenly, Miku materialized as Ms. Brown's avatar in her blank white staging room. It wasn't all that different from what it looked like in her own VR setup or in the *HyperBlast* game. She looked around and then quickly selected the spinning orb icon and opened the teacher dashboard, revealing numerous items that she'd never seen in her student VR menu. The dashboard items included sections labeled "Student Attendance Records," "Disciplinary Reviews," and even "Test Scores." Her mind reeled at the amount of sensitive information at her fingertips, and, for a second, the gravity of the situation settled on her like a thick, heavy blanket.

She normally would never do something this drastic in pursuit of a story. But what she'd seen in *HyperBlast* deserved a drastic response, and she needed to prove she wasn't making it up. Although now, seeing all of this information laid out in front of her, she realized just how risky and dangerous her plan really was. Miku took a deep breath and tried to calm her racing heart. She told herself this was the only way and thought: *What would Eleanor do?* So Miku continued to navigate through the menu and was careful not to give into temptation and peek, skipping over the folders carefully. Intruding on her classmates' privacy wasn't her goal; she was looking for a clue to whatever Principal Peterson was hiding.

"How're we looking out there?" Miku asked her real-world friends.

"Fine, just hurry up!" Tessa said, her voice soft and muffled to Miku's ears under the helmet.

Miku kept scrolling until she came to a folder labeled "VR Captures." Miku's heart started beating even faster. She opened the folder and saw rows upon rows of subfolders, broken out by source. Miku scrolled through captures from every VR event in the school: Eleanor's disastrous first social studies class, Mr. Okafor's second-period English, Life Sciences, Language Arts, Family and Consumer Sciences, Performing Arts, and finally *HyperBlast*.

Pay dirt. Miku scrolled through a school year's worth of videos and ended with the *HyperBlast* capture from that very morning. Miku selected the file and was met with a large red X floating before her.

"Access denied," said the automated voice. "This file is only viewable through administrative portals."

"Where are the administrative portals?" Miku asked the voice.

Outside her helmet, Miku heard Tessa and Raji cry out something in muffled exasperation.

"The administrative portals are located in Principal Peterson's Office and the Teachers' Lounge," replied the automated voice.

Miku navigated to the menu, brought up the school map feature, and located the Teachers' Lounge. It wasn't a real physical place in the school, at least not anymore. Mr. Okafor said that the previous real-world lounge had been replaced with racks of servers and miscellaneous cleaning supplies. The new Teachers' Lounge was a virtual space unseen by student eyes and mostly the stuff of legend and rumor. Teachers never discussed it; and, in fact, at times they even denied its existence when faced with some of the more outrageous rumors, but there it was—in plain sight on the official virtual map. Miku never understood why adults would deny something that was objectively provable if there wasn't something to hide. Miku had tried to run an article a month or two ago on the lounge in *The Beacon* because of all the stories that were flying around the halls and on the boards, and Mr. Peterson hadn't liked that.

Miku clicked on the Teachers' Lounge icon and held her breath. The blank staging room around her began to swirl, and then was reconstructed into a wide, airy space. She watched with a mix of excitement and confusion when, in the distance, swaying green palm trees began populating a breezy beach scene. *What kind of lounge is this?* she thought. Next, white marble columns sprouted up to a high trellised ceiling, interlaced with grapevines, a bright sun, and fluffy clouds above peeking through them.

She kind of expected a musty office with a mini-fridge, coffee-maker, and maybe some stale donuts in the corner, but this looked more like a high-class Italian villa. She glanced around as more details started to appear in her view. Walls began to materialize around the outside of the marble columns, which created a sort of indoor, open-air dining area. High-top tables began to dot the space, then a gaudy mirrored bar formed at one end, while, at the other, a dance floor and DJ booth appeared. Now the Teachers' Lounge resembled something that Miku had seen in movies that took place in Las Vegas casinos or maybe what dance clubs looked like in real life, she supposed. Then she heard the faint sound of pulsing dance music, which was starting to grow louder by the second, as other teachers' avatars started coming into view.

This wasn't what she was expecting at all and she definitely hadn't planned on running into faculty on her mission.

Panicking, Miku realized that in Ms. Brown's avatar she'd stick out like a recently fired thumb. She ducked behind a large potted tropical fern after it materialized—hoping to avoid detection.

"What's going on, Miku?" Tessa said, her voice muffled.

"It's a dance club!" Miku whispered back, covering the helmet's microphone with her hand. "The lounge is, like, a tropical disco, and the teachers are just milling around, *socializing*."

It was true; around the club Miku saw a handful of her teachers and some that she recognized as those who taught the eighth graders. Some were chatting at the standing tables, and a couple sat at the bar sipping virtual Shirley Temples, while the sixth-grade art teacher was positively cutting it up on the dance floor. Miku's blood ran cold as she caught a glimpse of the two avatars she was hoping *not* to run into standing under an awning, deep in conversation: Principal Peterson and Coach Tasker. Their heads were bent toward each other and they were looking quite conspiratorial from Miku's perspective. Thankfully, they were so engrossed in whatever they were talking about that they didn't seem to be paying any attention to anyone else in the club. This was her chance to get by them unnoticed.

Miku accessed her glowing ball menu, selected the Help icon, and whispered, "Locate administrative portal."

The menu collapsed and reformed into the glowing ball, which spun for a moment before zipping off through the club. It sped through obstacles and avatars alike, invisible to everyone but Miku. Then it stopped abruptly just above a coat check closet, illuminating the doorway below it. The closet was about a hundred paces along the wall where she was currently sheltering behind the fern; she could get to it almost entirely unseen, except for a small stretch where she'd be out in the open for only a few moments if she was quick. Miku took one last look at Mr. Peterson and Coach Tasker, who were still absorbed in their conversation, and then made a break for it.

She stood up and quickly moved her avatar along the outer wall of the club, walking briskly, but not so fast that she would arouse suspicion—she hoped. The teachers were busy going about their business, enjoying a break from their students and paying little attention to the others in the club. The ornate marble columns separated a walkway from the dining area and gave Miku cover if she walked along the outside. She was close to the closet door now but still needed to cross the open stretch in front of the kitchen that would briefly put her in the direct line of sight of Coach Tasker. Miku kept her head forward and eyes on the door, when—

Crash!

A server carrying a platter of dishes had walked right into her! Why were there animated servers in a club that couldn't serve real food!? The metal clanging was jarring and caused all the teacher avatars to stop and take notice; several stood up from their tables to get a better look. Miku bent down to help the fake server pick the plates off the floor. She grabbed a silver serving tray and shielded her face from Peterson and Tasker, who were now looking her way. She stayed low and ducked behind the last marble column next to the coat check closet.

With her back to the column, Miku flung the silver tray like a Frisbee in the opposite direction from the door. It sailed through the air and clattered onto the floor several yards away. It provided enough of a distraction for Miku to bolt the last few feet and quietly slip into the closet.

She closed the door quietly and pressed her back to it, looking around the tiny closet. Before her stood a man in a crushed velvet suit and black bow tie, standing straight and tall with his hands behind his back and a vacant smile plastered on his face. *This is pretty creepy if you ask me,* Miku thought.

"H-hello?" Miku offered, waving her hands in front of the man.

"Hello!" the man said cordially. Only his mouth moved; the rest of his body was fixed in place, and his eyes stared forward like those of a mannequin. *Very extra creepy.*

"Are you the administrative portal?" Miku asked, remembering that she was in a simulation, but still feeling slightly unnerved by the figure.

"Yes," the man answered.

"Okay. I'd like to access this morning's *HyperBlast* videos, please."

"What did the gazelle say to the tiger?"

"Huh?" Miku said. She felt a bead of sweat start to form, and her heart started to pick up speed. She didn't have time for this.

"What did the gazelle say to the tiger?" the man repeated implacably.

"Um, is this like a passcode kind of a thing?"

The man emitted an error sound, shaking his head, and again repeated, "What did the gazelle say to the tiger?"

"Miku, hurry up!" Tessa said, tugging on Miku's arm. "Lunch period is almost over!"

Miku's heartbeat, having already set records that day, quickened yet again. She looked around the bare closet, and at the oddly specific fake wood paneling on the walls, and at this strange gatekeeper to Principal Peterson's secrets.

Wait. Principal Peterson, Miku thought. *He is the clue.* This was programmed by Principal Peterson. What had Ms. Brown said the day she left? Miku's mind raced as she tried to remember everything she could about that moment.

"Sorry, can't eat, I've got to run," Miku said with a smile. Thank you, Ms. Brown.

The administrative portal smiled and waved his hand, revealing a large screen and console. File directories and folders populated the screen; some files she recognized, like "Security Footage" and "Yearly Budget," but many were labeled unintelligibly, like "Sqialix20," "Avz52giq#oz," and "^7burt&." Miku couldn't tell if the files were encrypted or just gibberish, but she didn't have time to puzzle it out.

She scanned through until at last landing at a *HyperBlast* folder; it seemed only certain files had been locked away here. One of them was the footage from that morning. Miku accessed the file, and the screen buzzed to life. She quickly muted the volume and dragged the playback bar to the end of the match.

Miku watched as Conrad stalked her during the BlastOff. She watched herself, in bush form, dodge his shots and, in a final act of defiance, catch his perfectly thrown HyperBall— *that looked pretty cool*, she thought to herself. She saw her teammates start to celebrate and then evaporate. And then she watched Coach Tasker descend from the sky and change the outcome of the BlastOff and the game.

"I knew it," Miku hissed in an angry whisper. "I caught that ball!"

"What?" came Raji's muffled response. "That's impossible!"

"And irrelevant!" Tessa yelled. "Time's up. Miku, get out of there!"

As if to reinforce the urgency of the situation, there was suddenly a loud knock at the coat check closet door.

Coach Tasker's voice came muffled through the door. "Who's in there?" Another round of knocking. "That portal is for authorized personnel only!"

Miku frantically closed the playback video, but she couldn't leave without evidence—she'd seen too much, and she needed to be able to prove to Eleanor that something really was going on. She grabbed her avatar's glowing ball icon and opened the teacher dashboard. The knocking at the door grew to a heavy banging as she clicked on the email icon and created a new message. Hurriedly, she began selecting files and folders from administrative portal and dragging them into her open email.

There was only so much information that would fit, so, first, she grabbed the *HyperBlast* footage from that morning, and then just started selecting whatever files and folders she could, dragging it all into the email. The banging at the door was getting even more pronounced now, and there were other voices that Miku could hear on the other side of the door while Tessa and Raji were tugging furiously at her body, trying to get her out of the simulation. Miku quickly selected the email's recipient field, tapped out an address, and hit Send before pulling the helmet off her head.

Just then, the door to the coat check closet finally gave way and burst open, along with Coach Tasker, who tumbled in shoulder first. She grunted and spun with almost inhuman reflexes as she searched for the intruder, and as Principal Peterson stood at the door, peering in. Instead of an intruder, they only found the placid smile of the man in the crushed velvet suit.

"What did the gazelle say to the tiger?" he asked.

CHAPTER 9
SCANDAL!

ELEANOR'S PHONE, A beat-up, off-brand smartphone that was several years old at this point, dinged to notify her that she had a new email. The sender was *RBrown@brightonMS.edu*. The subject line and the body of the message were empty, but attached to it were reams of documents, spreadsheets, and more than a few videos.

This must be Miku, Eleanor thought as she scrolled through the rather haphazardly and cryptically labeled attachments. After scanning a few at random, she opened a spreadsheet simply titled "Reimbursements." Eleanor's eyes widened as she looked down row after row of what could only be financial records. This was definitely from Miku.

ELEANOR: Miku, what did you email me!?

ELEANOR: What are these docs?

MIKU: Proof! Peterson, Conrad and Tasker are fixing HyperBlast games!

ELEANOR: Um, these show WAY more than that

MIKU: What do you mean?

ELEANOR: Miku, they prove that there is a criminal conspiracy between Peterson and SuperInteliCom.

MIKU: Wait, wut?

ELEANOR: Peterson is selling private student info!

ELEANOR: He's data-mining, I knew it!!!

MIKU: Wow . . . but . . .

MIKU: what about Conrad???

ELEANOR: What about him?

MIKU: He's in on it too, right?

MIKU: He's an evil genius?

ELEANOR: Miku, at most Conrad is a pawn.

ELEANOR: What you found is proof that goes all the way to the top! And maybe then some. This could even put the school board in some very hot water.

MIKU: Oh

ELEANOR: By the way, Miku, where on earth did you get the docs?

MIKU: You know, reporting!

MIKU: Just normal investigation stuff!

Eleanor took a breath and held it. It had been a few days since Miku had sent her the email evidence. Since then, a lot had happened, and Eleanor was about to tell the world about it. The red light in her studio turned green and the microphone went live, beaming her signal to millions of listeners.

"We're back with *The Whole Story*. I'm your host, Eleanor Amplified. I've got an *important* update to my investigation of the mysterious tech company SuperInteliCom.

"Listeners will remember my suspicion of the company doubled after I was nearly blown up in a factory explosion of a subsidiary company called SmartFüdz only a week ago. Well, I recently obtained evidence implicating SuperInteliCom in some real criminal activity: covert data mining, also known as illegally collecting users' private information, or, in this case, the private data of Brighton Middle School students.

"Two nights ago, I presented the evidence to the Brighton School Board and asked if they had anything to comment, and they were appalled. The Board assured me this was unsanctioned activity and that they were not aware of Principal Marvin Peterson's actions despite the Board's full support of Peterson's new partnership with the tech company that had been presented at the start of the year. They promised full transparency and swift action. To that end, Principal Marvin Peterson has been fired. The school's technology and nutrition programs, the main sources of the data-mining activity, have ended.

"Perhaps unsurprisingly, I've still been unable to track down any representative for SuperInteliCom. After all of the trouble they have caused, I'm beginning to wonder if the company even exists or is only a front for another entity attempting to hide *its* identity. I'll keep digging, listeners, but at least for now, know that Brighton Middle School is safe. This has been another edition of *The Whole Story*. For my producer, Barry Cunningham, and editor, Arthur Richman, I'm Eleanor Amplified. Until next time, listeners."

The theme music for *The Whole Story* played through Eleanor's headset, the green light in the ceiling turned red again, and then the room lights switched on.

"Great show, Eleanor," Barry said over the intercom.

Eleanor said nothing but removed her headphones and sat, resting her chin on her fist. She knew there were too many unanswered questions. What was the deal with the SmartFüdz factory, and how did all those weird, exotic plants fit into this story? And maybe more important, what happened to the creepy Gilmin Midrovia, and his rather large accomplice? Miku had been right about everything so far, and Eleanor knew there was a good chance the answers she needed would still be found at Brighton Middle.

Mr. Richman entered the studio a moment later, although not with his usual gusto. He slumped down in a seat across the table from Eleanor, locking eyes with her. The two remained that way for a full minute, before Mr. Richman broke the silence.

"We're thinking the same thing."

"This isn't sitting right," Eleanor said after a moment, staring back across at her boss.

"Correct."

"I didn't finish the job at the school."

"Uh huh."

"I've got to go back."

"Yep."

Eleanor exhaled, then smacked her hands on the top of the table before standing up. "Right!" she said as she began gathering her things. Barry came into the studio with his head buried in papers and rundowns for upcoming shows.

"Eleanor, we've got to record some promos for WBER, that little station up north. Oh, and have you prepped for your interview with the Sultan of—"

Barry stopped, realizing that his colleagues had come to a resolute decision moments ago without him.

"Did I miss something?" Barry asked, cognizant as ever of their looming deadlines and demanding broadcast schedule.

"I'm going back to the school, Barry," Eleanor said. "The investigation's not over." She grabbed her jacket from the back of her chair.

"That reminds me," Barry said. "I heard back from the laboratory about the soup sample."

"*Now* you're reminded, Barry?" Eleanor asked, somewhat incredulous. "What was the analysis, what'd we learn?"

"That's just it, Eleanor," Barry said. "It was inconclusive. It was mostly just a very well-made tomato soup, except for *one ingredient*."

"Aaaaaaand?" Eleanor said expectantly.

"Yeah, Barry, cut the suspense. What was the ingredient, *love*?" Mr. Richman added.

"They don't know. It's nontoxic, but it doesn't appear in any scientific literature."

"Super helpful, thanks, Barry," Eleanor said sarcastically.

"That's why I didn't mention it!" Barry said, throwing his arms up and in the process accidentally tossing his papers around the studio. "They're going to call me back soon with more information."

"Good," Eleanor grumbled. "Call me when they do. But I think I already know the answer."

"Will do," Barry said as he knelt down to pick up his scattered papers.

"I've still got to find some shred of evidence as to who is behind SuperInteliCom," Eleanor continued. "It's not like finding information on them before was easy, but now the company has up and vanished after the school board got wind of it." Eleanor started to pace a little in the small studio. "Same for SmartFüdz. The school is still the only lead I have."

"And, Eleanor," Mr. Richman said, "don't forget to check in with Miku. The kid's got a nose for trouble, and she probably knows more than she thinks she does."

"Aye, aye, Chief," Eleanor said, slinging her pack over her shoulder. "Now that Principal Peterson is gone, she should at least be enjoying seventh grade a little more."

....

The midday sun was glaring down on the school grounds as Eleanor strode through Brighton's front doors, the engraved words DISCAT COGITARE, COGITARE VIVERE shining overhead. Despite the sun, she still felt a lingering chill breeze, and buttoned her coat. It had only been a few days, but she couldn't help feeling a little excited to be back, especially now that she'd exposed Peterson's scheme. It was like checking on the progress of a garden that she'd helped weed and seed back to health.

Except that it seemed like this garden had suddenly dried out and gone fallow. As warm and bright as the sun was outside, inside there was only gloom and despair. The few kids walking the halls looked pale and ghostly; litter lined the floors and was piling up around overstuffed trash bins; an X was spray-painted maliciously over one of the BRIGHTON UP YOUR DAY! posters that remained on the walls. Eleanor walked through the hallways confused about what could've happened to make such a drastic change at the school in only a few days. As she walked, she saw Mr. Okafor's nameplate on a classroom door and peeked in the window. Inside, he was lecturing a class of clearly tired, unhappy-looking youngsters, but there was no sign of a VR helmet or ZipTab in sight. Instead, he was writing something at the blackboard, and there were books on each student's desk.

Eleanor continued walking, trying to remember her way around the maze of hallways, until she found herself at the office of *The Brighton Beacon*. There was no window in this door, so she knocked twice before she entered, leaving the door open a crack behind her. Inside, Miku sat alone at a drafting table with a mockup of the latest *Beacon* edition in front of her. The front-page headline read *"Brighton Beacon* No More."

"Hi, Miku," Eleanor said gently.

"Hi, Eleanor," Miku said without looking up. She sniffled and let out a sad sigh. "*The Beacon* is shutting down."

"I can see that," Eleanor said. "What happened?"

"I don't know," Miku said with a shrug. "As soon as Peterson left, Mr. Okafor said we lost funding." She lifted the papers in her hands weakly. "I guess this is what winning looks like, huh?"

"What do you mean, Miku?"

Miku looked at the half-packed boxes and piles of old newspapers around the office and shrugged again, but Eleanor could tell there was something else.

"Miku," Eleanor said as she pulled up a chair and sat down at the drafting table, "reporting isn't about winning or losing. I don't cover a story to *win*."

"That's easy for you to say!" Miku said, standing and waving a hand at Eleanor, her temper flaring. "You're so good at it! You always beat the bad guys!"

"Wrong! I expose facts," Eleanor said, feeling herself become upset as well. "I bring bad behavior to light, and I hold people in power accountable. Because, let me tell you, Miku, the only thing the bad guys need is opportunity. There's always going to be a villain, or sometimes just a jerk, who tries to take advantage of the rest of us. And do you know how they do it? In the shadows. In the dark, where no one can see what they're up to, and no one knows about it, and that's where we come in. We shine a light on their wrongdoing so they can't keep getting away with it.

"But it's not just about catching bad guys, Miku, it's about making things fair and safe for all of us. You, me, the people of Brighton, the citizens of Union City . . . we're a community. And people within communities might have different opinions and different ideas, but we have to have the same information, and the same facts, so that we can think intelligently about how to make our community better. And without common ground, or at least just a shared reality, a community—no, a *society*—it can't work."

"So the point is to make things better?" Miku said pointedly.

"That's usually how it goes."

"Then why is everything *worse*?!" Miku shouted before collapsing back into her chair.

Then, just like someone had flipped a switch, the fiery energy drained out of Miku. She sniffed again, and Eleanor looked at her, remembering that, although Miku was very mature for her age, she was still only twelve years old.

Eleanor waited for a moment and then said softly, "I'm sorry, can we start over?"

Miku nodded.

"Okay. What happened? Why are things worse?"

"For starters, everyone is still *miserable*," Miku began. "The school is still divided; there's a lot of gossip, kids no longer trust one another, and the ABCs and Conrad are still bullying people behind the scenes."

"Well, isn't part of that just part of growing up and being in school?" Eleanor asked, but just as she did, she remembered one of her first run-ins with bullies—serious bullies.

"You know," Eleanor began, "back in high school a couple bullies almost got me expelled."

"Really?" Miku said, disbelieving. "*You?*"

"Yeah. They were a brother and sister—twins, actually. I thought they were my friends, but they framed me for a prank that *they* committed, and they did it to cover up the fact that *they* were trying to cheat and get better grades. And they nearly got away with it. My mom was furious."

"What did you do?"

"I investigated! I uncovered their plot, got a whole bunch of evidence, and then I put it all out there in front of the whole school."

"Wow," Miku said. "And was it better after that?"

"Sort of," Eleanor said. "They switched schools. I never saw them again. But school went back to normal."

"That's what I mean!" Miku said forcefully. "This school hasn't gone back to normal. It's still *different*."

"It's only been days since Peterson was removed," Eleanor said optimistically. "Plus, the social network was just shut down, SmartFüdz is out, no more ZipTabs, no more VR classes . . ."

"Yeah, but—"

"And what about *HyperBlast*?" Eleanor said, jumping in.

"*HyperBlast* is still here," Miku explained, looking downcast. "It was too popular to get rid of."

"Oh, well, we got most of it, right?" Eleanor said, still trying to get Miku to see the bright side. "Maybe it's taking a little time for the school culture to change? Things don't just happen overnight."

"Eleanor, we *missed* something. I think there's something else happening at Brighton."

"Well, it's possible, and I'm willing to believe there could be, but we need more evidence," Eleanor said. "Is there anything else you're not telling me?"

"Well, there's Conrad," Miku said, looking down and letting her hair cover her face a little.

"Right. Miku, sometimes people are just mean and need to grow up a bit—"

"He wasn't mean before," Miku interrupted, looking Eleanor dead in the eye. "He was my friend. More than that, to me, anyway . . ." Miku trailed off then as her cheeks turned a soft pink.

"What? How? Huh?" Eleanor said, disbelieving.

"He changed," Miku said, still looking down.

Then Miku told Eleanor the story of how she and Conrad first met.

She was new to Brighton; her family had moved into their apartment the week just before classes started. The apartment was in a complex on the border of the school district, across a busy road that separated it from an older neighborhood of big stone houses and quiet streets. Miku had lived in a lot of apartment complexes and didn't mind them so much because they were easier to move in and out of, given her folks' jobs.

Miku had woken up early the first day of classes, having already packed her books and supplies and gone over her schedule the night before. Sitting around the new apartment among all the boxes made her anxious, so she grabbed her backpack and a book she was reading and set out for the bus stop. Miku left her apartment complex and crossed the busy road in front. She walked down the other side of the road a few yards and stopped in front of a large stone entrance that read COUNCIL CREEK ESTATES. It was the entrance to a quiet neighborhood of large, stately stone houses.

She'd shown up early, probably too early, on that cool September morning, so she opened her book and began reading. As Miku stood, reading, she realized that someone was walking toward her. Out of the corner of her eye, she could see a boy, roughly her age, had stopped and was standing a few feet from her. She closed her book and looked off down the road, pretending to possibly see the bus on the horizon if she craned her neck just right.

"It won't be here for another twenty-two minutes," he said.

"That's precise," Miku said.

"It's predictable."

"And how do you know, anyway?"

"The same way I know it's about to rain," the boy said with an easy smile.

Miku had stopped being friendly to new people at her last school, where she'd been labeled as "desperate for friends" after she tried talking to a clique of cool kids. In truth, she probably had tried too hard—a couple jokes definitely didn't land as intended—but she had only been trying to meet people. After that incident she resolved to never again be overly friendly. She'd rather be left alone than laughed at.

Commuters flew up and down the road, but there was no sign of any school bus. A minute later, the gray skies turned darker and a light rain started falling. The boy pulled out an umbrella from his bag and opened it. Miku's umbrella was still packed away in some box and probably under a stack of other boxes. She hunched up her backpack and put her book under her arm, trying to keep it from getting wet.

"It always rains when the cold wind blows across the lake like it did this morning," the boy said, and then motioned with his umbrella. "I've got room under here."

"I'm fine," she replied.

More cars whizzed past, kicking up spray from the road. The rain got heavier. If the boy was right about the bus, she'd be drenched by the time it got there.

"Okay, yes, if you wouldn't mind," Miku said, rushing over to the boy, who moved his arm over, allowing Miku underneath.

"You're new here?" he said.

"Yeah, we just moved in over there, across the road, in the apartments."

"Oh, I live over there," he said, motioning into the neighborhood, toward a tall, nice-looking colonial about a block away. The front porch light was on, some bikes rested against the garage door, and there was a tire swing hung from a tree in the side yard. Miku could always spot a house that had been lived in for a long time, because she'd never had one.

"Is that the Heimler biography you're reading?" he asked, nodding to the book Miku was clutching.

"Yeah! You know it?" Miku said with surprise.

Alfred Heimler was an inventor and philanthropist, best known for creating the prestigious Heimler Award for Journalism. Miku had picked up the hardback edition after critics gushed about it in the papers. She usually liked reading about historical figures—especially journalists—but, so far, she didn't love it.

"I read it," the boy said, "but, honestly, I didn't really like it."

"Me neither!" Miku blurted out. "I mean, I just started it, and it got such good reviews, but Heimler sounds like kind of a—"

"Sleazebag," the boy and Miku said at the same time, causing them both to giggle.

"I haven't met someone my age who likes reading biographies," the boy said, looking at her with a smile and extending his hand. "I'm Conrad."

"I'm Miku." She smiled back.

The two of them shook hands, and when the bus came exactly nineteen minutes later, they shared a seat in the back and chatted all the way to school. Conrad was handsome, but unpretentious and very approachable—welcoming even. His sense of humor was dry and understated, but it fit quite well with Miku's—at times intense—earnestness. They had a lot in common: an interest in politics and the news, an uncanny knack for following details, and a driving sense of ambition. They became fast friends, even though their social circles at Brighton didn't really overlap. After a few months, Miku started *The Brighton Beacon*, with the help of Mr. Okafor, while Conrad got involved with student government and sports. Despite their differing interests, the two always made time for each other to catch up, commiserate about being in sixth grade, and share dreams for the future.

"The last time I talked to him—really talked to him—was last summer," Miku said. "He was about to go meet the new principal because he wanted to run for class president."

"What do you mean?" Eleanor asked. "Then what happened?"

"The Conrad I knew never came back. The person who did was cold, mean. I don't think anyone else noticed; he was still clever and funny, but his jokes were cruel. And he acted like he didn't even know me."

"Wow," Eleanor said in a stunned whisper. "I'm sorry, Miku."

"It's okay," she replied after a moment. "The worst part is that eventually it wasn't just Conrad; it was the whole school. Students here changed after the curriculum changed, and I was so positive it was Peterson's fault!"

"Again, it's possible, but—"

"Eleanor," Miku shouted, "something has happened, and I need you to help me fix it! We need to find a way to fix the school *and* Conrad. He was my best friend before all of this happened, and I want him back. Eleanor, I need to tell him that I—"

Suddenly a blood-curdling scream from the office door cut Miku off.

Eleanor and Miku jumped, startled, and turned to see Conrad as he lurched into the room, holding his head in agony. He took two steps and twisted as his legs buckled, sending him sprawling on his back on the floor. Eleanor and Miku exchanged a perplexed glance, and then dashed to his aid. Eleanor checked his vital signs and to make sure that he hadn't hit his head too hard as Miku grabbed an old mug of tea from the desk, then splashed the contents on his face.

"Miku!" Eleanor cried.

"Sorry," Miku said, realizing now that maybe that wasn't the best thing to do in that moment. "They always do it in the movies, so I thought it would work."

Eleanor started to say something, but then Conrad sputtered and his eyes fluttered open. He glanced at Eleanor and then at Miku, confusion etched on his face.

"Miku?" he asked, breathing heavily. "What . . . happened?"

CHAPTER 10
THE RUMPUS ROOM

MIKU STARED AT Conrad, feeling a mixture of relief, confusion, and a few other emotions that, all too quickly, transformed into anger.

"You tell us what happened, weirdo!" Miku shouted as she kneeled down as if to grab him. "You're the one making the horror movie entrance!"

"Miku, give him a minute," Eleanor said, gesturing for her to take a step back. She knew no one could fake this kind of distress, not even the smug preteen influencer, and, after seeing Conrad's pale complexion, confused look, and watery eyes, she knew that something was wrong.

"But, Eleanor—" Miku started, but Eleanor waved her back again and paired it with a stern look.

"No, it's okay, Ms. Agrandar," Conrad said weakly as he tried to sit upright. "I was watching you from the door." He rubbed his head and, in the process, mussed up his signature floppy hairstyle. "No, I wasn't watching, I was spying . . ." he said slowly like each memory was a piece of a puzzle he was trying to put together. "I was spying on you . . . for *Coach Tasker*!" he said frantically, turning to Eleanor and Miku.

Eleanor and Miku glanced at each other and then back at Conrad. He sounded distraught, even slightly hysterical, and not at all the cool-as-a-cucumber boy that Eleanor had come to know over the last few days or that Miku had seen over the last school year.

Miku gave Eleanor another look, then stood, watching Conrad with suspicion. "Continue," she said, folding her arms.

"I was supposed to gather information on you . . . and Ms. Agrandar," Conrad said as he pointed at Eleanor with a look that said even he was surprised by the things coming out of his mouth.

"I don't know why or what she wants, but I have to do what she says. Or at least I had to until—"

"I knew Coach Tasker was in on it!" Miku said, slapping a fist into her palm.

"In on *what*?" Eleanor said with exasperation, feeling like they were raising just as many questions as they were answering.

"It!" Miku shot back, throwing her arms in the air. "The royal 'it,' Eleanor; the scheme, the plot, the nefariousness!"

"But nothing in those documents you uncovered implicated Tasker!" Eleanor retorted. "Conrad, you have to tell us what you know."

"It's all so fuzzy . . . I can't remember everything. It's like I've been in a game of *HyperBlast* for months."

"Wait, why is he talking about *HyperBlast*?" Eleanor asked, glancing at Miku.

However, Miku didn't hear her because she was intent on pressing him for as much information as she could get while he was willing to give it up. "What about Tasker?" Miku asked Conrad. "What's she up to?"

"And what about Peterson?" Eleanor chimed in. "He was stealing students' data! Wasn't he?"

Conrad waved them away and tried to stand up a few times before finally succeeding with a little bit of help from Miku. He gave her a small smile and then looked around uneasily as he brushed off his fashionable clothes—which he now seemed oddly uncomfortable wearing. He looked at the door to the hall and then at the PA speaker in the corner of the room, before leaning in toward Miku and Eleanor.

"Not here," he whispered.

Miku and Eleanor caught his meaning and nodded, but Miku wasn't about to let him off easily—she needed some answers.

"Tonight," she whispered back. "I'll call Raji and Tessa. This calls for all hands on deck."

"Where?" Eleanor said quietly. "I'd volunteer, but my apartment is, ah, on the small side."

Miku shook her head as Eleanor looked at her. "My parents would be on top of us at my place!"

"We can use my house," Conrad offered quietly. "We've got a rec room that's pretty private."

"Rec room?" Miku replied. "You mean your 'rumpus room'?"

Eleanor tried not to laugh, and it came out as a snort.

"What? No, that's a silly name," Conrad said, looking embarrassed.

"No, no, that's what your mom called it," Miku whispered back. "Last year, anyway."

Conrad shook his head, his voice a little louder than before. "I don't think so."

"No, definitely," Miku replied a litter louder than him. "There is a foosball table, the beanbag chairs, all those movie posters—"

"It's a rec room now!" Conrad interrupted firmly.

"Fine!" Miku shot back.

"Hey!" Eleanor hissed, already sick of their bickering. "Can we *focus*?"

Miku and Conrad looked bashfully at Eleanor, and Miku mouthed an apology.

"Okay," Eleanor continued quietly, "tonight, eight o'clock, at Conrad's house. I'll bring pizza."

"Agreed," Conrad said, holding out his hand for Miku to shake.

"Okay," Miku said simply, ignoring his hand. "See you tonight."

....

At 7:58 p.m. Miku was sitting on the curb outside her apartment entrance, facing the parking lot that emptied onto the busy road. They had decided that Raji and Tessa would take the bus to her place, and then they'd all walk to Conrad's house together. The only problem was that Raji and Tessa were late. Miku tapped her foot on the pavement and looked around. She'd waited inside for as long as she could, but her excitement and anxiety had finally gotten the better of her—she needed some fresh air. Ever since this afternoon, her head had been swirling. Could Conrad really be different now? Had something happened that made him act like such a jerk? What did that mean for their friendship? The questions kept buzzing around in her head, and she didn't know how to make them stop.

Finally, the number 82 bus squeaked to a stop at the entrance to Miku's apartment complex as cars continued to rush by. The doors opened, and Tessa and Raji bounded down the steps as Miku rose from where she'd been sitting to meet them.

"Are you ready for this?" Tessa asked Miku.

"I guess I have to be," Miku replied, zipping up her hoodie.

Raji folded his arms. "Well, I don't like it."

"What a shock," Tessa said, sounding not at all surprised; then she and Miku looked at each other and smiled. Typical Raji.

They waited for a gap in the traffic on the busy road in front of her apartment complex, and then made brief small talk as they walked the few yards down the sidewalk toward the stone entrance of Council Creek Estates. The evening sky was turning a stunning mix of purple and red as the sun sank to the horizon. Raji and Tessa lived on the opposite end of town from Miku, in a newer development of small, efficient, single-family homes, so the three felt a little intimidated walking through the neighborhood of large, well-groomed houses where many of Brighton's lawyers and doctors lived. Raji stuffed his hands in his pockets and chewed on his lip while Tessa and Miku marveled at the manicured lawns, rocks walls, and tall maples. In a moment, they came to the house with a tire swing in the front yard, although it looked like no one had used it in ages. Miku led Tessa and Raji along the driveway to the back of the house, where a door led to the basement room.

Miku had barely knocked once when Conrad flung open the door and rushed them into the basement. It was exactly as Miku remembered it: old movie posters lined the walls, and next to the foosball table were two cedar cabinets stuffed with board games. In the middle of the room sat an octagonal card table, next to the old, lumpy couch and beanbag chairs in front of the TV.

"Now *this* is a rumpus room," Miku said.

"Don't start," Conrad said, rolling his eyes. "It feels like forever since I've even been down here. *In the rec room.*"

"I didn't know they still made shag carpet," Raji said, inspecting the green rug beneath their feet.

Then another knock came at the basement door. As expected, when Conrad opened it, in walked Eleanor, followed by Mr. Okafor, who was holding several pizzas.

"Mr. Okafor!" Miku said, surprised. "How did you know—"

"I invited him," Eleanor said. "*And* I explained the situation to him."

"And I'm glad you did, Eleanor. Although I should've guessed you weren't a real sub," Mr. Okafor said, setting the pizzas down on the card table.

"Um, is everyone okay with Conrad learning Eleanor's true identity?" Raji asked, looking around the room.

"That she's really Eleanor Amplified, the famous reporter?" Conrad replied, causing a brief pause and heads to turn. "Between the news of the data theft and Principal Peterson getting fired, I figured it out."

"I suppose the cat is out of the bag," Eleanor said.

"It's less to explain," Mr. Okafor said easily, "How're you feeling, Conrad, after your *episode*?"

"Better. But also weirder," Conrad said, scratching his head. "Can we jump on this pizza before this gets started? I'm starving."

"Agreed!" Raji said and began flipping open pizza boxes. The group grabbed slices—even Miku, as Eleanor had considerately ordered one gluten-free, tomato pie—and took seats around the card table. The food was a welcome diversion from the incredibly awkward situation: for months Conrad had been Miku and the Newsers' tormenter; their archenemy. Now he was hosting them in his rumpus room.

Eleanor and Mr. Okafor couldn't help but feel the tension in the room and tried to break it.

Mr. Okafor began by stating the obvious. "So, Conrad, Eleanor tells me it seems you might have been hypnotized for the better part of a year."

Conrad grimaced and stammered out, "I . . . well, yeah, I guess so."

"And that's why you've been such a jerk," Eleanor continued.

"Whoa, Eleanor, he is just a kid!" Mr. Okafor chided, although his tone suggested he agreed.

"Hey, I'm no teacher, remember?" Eleanor said. "Just an objective third party."

"She's right," Conrad said, putting down his slice of pizza and hanging his head. "I remember that much; and I was a total jerk."

"Big time," Tessa added.

"A monumental piece of cow plop," Raji tacked on, sensing his chance.

Conrad nodded sadly.

"Putting that aside for a moment," Miku jumped in, "can you tell us what happened to you?"

Conrad leaned back in his seat and looked around the table. Miku held his gaze for a moment, realizing that, for the first time in a long while, his eyes weren't cold. He looked genuine, not scheming or malevolent. She began remembering those mornings the year before when they'd wait at the bus stop together. She would always arrive twenty or thirty minutes early, and he'd always show up minutes after. The memory made her smile, but then she quickly shook it away. There would be time to reminisce, and maybe talk to each other about what had happened between them, later. Right now, Miku needed answers.

"A lot of it is still foggy," Conrad began, "but it all started the morning I went to the school to meet with Principal Peterson."

"I knew it!" Miku blurted, before quickly clapping her hands over her mouth.

"I remember I woke up early that morning," Conrad continued. "I was nervous because Mr. Peterson wanted to talk to me, and I figured if I wanted to be class president, I'd better get along with the new principal. I went to the school and it was deserted—not a janitor, not a teacher, not even Mr. Funches in the lunchroom. This was back before the gym became the *HyperBlast* arena and before all the VR headsets and machines. It still looked normal.

"I went to Peterson's office, and there was a note on the door telling me to meet him in the library. So I went. It was still a working library then, not all closed up like it is now. He wasn't in the entryway, so I looked around a bit, but he wasn't anywhere in the main hall, so I figured maybe he was downstairs in archives. So I went down there and saw the door to the records room was ajar. There was some strange light coming out, too. But then, just as I was about to open the door, I felt this sting in my arm . . ." Conrad reflexively rubbed his upper arm, remembering the pain and shock of the moment. "And from then on, I was different."

The group stared back at him.

Eleanor and Mr. Okafor shared a look of concern while Miku rubbed her chin, considering what she'd heard. Raji and Tessa definitely weren't buying it, and they exchanged skeptical glances and shook their heads. Conrad watched them all and waited.

"Define *different*," Miku said.

"It was like . . . it felt like I was the only person in the world who mattered," Conrad said. "And I wanted to use the ZipTabs, and the boards, and my video feeds to create a place where everyone was paying attention to me and only me. Like I wanted to be the emperor of my own empire, sort of."

"What do you mean?" Eleanor said. "How did you just *decide* to create a social empire?"

"Mr. Peterson gave me codes to the ZipTabs," Conrad explained. "And I would use them to spread gossip. I erased posts, and I made stuff up. You name it. And everyone believed me because, well, I was all over the place." He looked down at his hands and looked ashamed.

"So Peterson was in on it!?" Miku exclaimed, pounding the table.

"Easy, Miku!" Conrad said, frantic. "My parents are upstairs!" Then he continued. "And, yes, I don't know exactly what 'it' is, but I do know that he was involved. And I know that he rigged the school election to make me class president, but what I don't know is why. I think I only ever spoke to him a couple times."

"I knew the election was a fraud," Miku said energetically, although slightly quieter than before.

"But wait; he wasn't giving you orders?" Eleanor asked.

"No," Conrad said with a shake of his head. "No one ordered me to do anything. They just helped me be awful."

"And by 'they,'" Mr. Okafor began, leaning forward on the card table and steepling his fingers, "you mean . . ."

"Coach Tasker," Miku said, just above a whisper.

"Yes."

"So Coach Tasker really did alter the *HyperBlast* match to let Conrad win?" Tessa asked. "Because I still don't remember it."

"She did," Conrad confirmed. "She hypnotized everyone with her red whistle and erased their memories. Everyone but Miku, that is. I've never seen her do that before."

"Why didn't she erase your memory?" Raji asked pointedly.

Conrad shrugged. "I was already hypnotized, I guess. And she needed me to win the game."

Eleanor mulled that over. "Do you think Principal Peterson knew about Coach Tasker's hypnotizing whistle?"

"Probably," Conrad replied.

"I saw Peterson and Tasker meeting in the Teachers' Lounge," Miku added. "They looked pretty suspicious."

"You saw what, *where*, Miku?" Mr. Okafor said. His easy smile had vanished. "In what way was it appropriate for you to be in the Teachers' Lounge?"

"Um, okay, I can explain," Miku started cautiously. "I borrowed Eleanor—er, Ms. Brown's VR helmet..."

"Miku, that is a serious violation!" Mr. Okafor said, his teacherly instincts leaving him unable to let the infraction slide.

"Adisa," Eleanor said, "if she hadn't violated the rules, we wouldn't know any of this."

"I suppose that's true," Mr. Okafor said, leaning back and folding his arms. "But I don't like my students thinking it's okay to break school rules. We'll be talking about this later, Miku."

Miku lowered her head and sank sullenly back in her seat. She hated getting on Mr. Okafor's bad side.

"It sounds to me like Coach Tasker and Principal Peterson broke the rules first," Eleanor replied.

"So you're telling us," Raji interrupted angrily, "that the principal and our gym teacher conspired to make you popular?" He looked accusingly at Conrad, who lowered his eyes, while Tessa grabbed Raji's arm to quiet him. "No, this is ridiculous!" Raji said, pulling his arm away. "What did Mr. Peterson and Coach Tasker gain by making everyone either scared or in love with you, Praeder?"

Just then, Eleanor's phone rang. She pulled it out of her satchel and then looked around the table. "Hang on, everyone. I've got to take this."

Miku watched as she got up and heard her say, "Barry, did you get the results?" Then Raji and Conrad's back-and-forth was all she could hear. She sat back in her chair and picked absentmindedly at a scratch on the table. Her thoughts were reeling: She believed Conrad's story, but what did that have to do with the data theft that Eleanor uncovered? Why did

Peterson and Tasker want to make Conrad into a bully—or an icon, depending on your point of view—and turn the school into such a mean place? Nothing was adding up.

In the corner of the room, Eleanor spoke in hushed tones to her producer. Whatever they were talking about, it was important. After a minute or two of conference, Eleanor ended the call, put her phone back in her bag, and returned to the table.

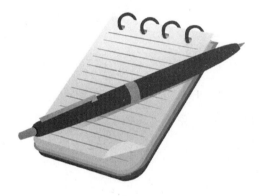

"What was that about?" Miku asked.

"I don't want to say right now," Eleanor answered, but I think I've connected some dots, and I've got a working theory of what's going on here."

"That's great," Miku said, "because we can't figure it out."

"Can't you illuminate anything?" Mr. Okafor asked.

"I'll explain everything, but first I'll need your help. *All of you.*"

"What can we do?" Raji asked.

"I need to know what's in that library, and I need evidence," Eleanor said. "Drat, I wish I hadn't broken my tape recorder."

"Why don't you use your phone?" Miku asked.

"My phone?" Eleanor asked in reply.

"Wow, she *is* hopeless," Raji said, causing the other kids around the table to chuckle.

"Let me see it," Tessa said, holding out her hand.

Eleanor opened her satchel and reluctantly handed Tessa her phone.

"What kind is it?" Miku asked.

"I . . . I'm not even sure," Tessa said, turning the smartphone over in her hands like an archaeologist who has stumbled upon evidence of an unknown civilization. "But it has a microphone, so it probably has the ability to record sound."

"Where did you find that thing?" Raji asked with wonder. "Is it, like, a prototype of what phones were supposed to turn into?"

"It's a *normal phone!*" Eleanor said, getting agitated. "Maybe it's a little old, I don't know. I think I got it at one of those stands in the mall years ago."

Miku, Raji, and Conrad gasped and were too stunned by Eleanor's purchasing methods to speak. Tessa, meanwhile, continued clicking through Eleanor's janky phone's settings. With a little effort she was able to download the necessary apps, and after a few more minutes of fiddling, she successfully enabled the phone to record. Tessa handed the phone back to Eleanor.

"Here. Now, the next time you want to record something, I configured it so you just have to press this button," Tessa said, indicating a button on the side of the phone. "It'll start right up."

"Hey, thanks!" Eleanor said, examining the phone.

"I also cleaned up your home screen and freed up some memory," Tessa added. "I mean, what little memory there was in the first place."

"Okay, *okay*! I know I need a new phone but—"

"Can we get back to how you're supposed to get anywhere near the library?" Raji interrupted.

"It'll be hard. Maybe impossible," Conrad said. "Tasker's got eyes all over the school. Cameras, bugs . . . I don't even know what else."

"And since you broke the story about Peterson, your cover is blown," Mr. Okafor said. "If you go to that library, you'll be cooked."

The group sat for a moment in silence. Principal Peterson

had been Brighton's face of authority, but Coach Tasker was legitimately feared. No one wanted to run afoul of her in normal circumstances, let alone be seen trying to expose her criminal conspiracy. And now that she apparently had the power to erase memories, Tasker was all the more terrifying.

"I've got an idea," Conrad offered. "Tomorrow's the big *HyperBlast* tournament."

"Another wonderful day at Brighton Middle," Raji scoffed.

"What about it, Conrad?" Eleanor asked.

"It's an all-day event. She'll have her hands full refereeing the matches. You might be able to sneak in unnoticed."

"Maybe," Miku said, sounding unconvinced. "But it's still risky. We don't see her or what she's doing half the time."

"True," Conrad agreed. "Which is why we might be able to create a distraction."

"Oh yeah?" Raji sneered. "Your Red Team destroys the Blue Team in a matter of minutes! That's not very distracting."

"Not if I level the playing field!" Conrad continued, throwing Raji a look. "I'm the one who chooses the game maps and leads the Red Team, remember?"

"If Conrad undermines the Red Team, then we might have a chance of extending the match, and keeping her attention on us," Miku said, catching on.

"Wait," Tessa interjected, "we are forgetting something crucial. What about Tasker's hypno-whistle? Aren't we putting ourselves in danger?"

"Well, we'd have to be careful," Conrad said. "It couldn't be obvious we were trying to distract her."

"Last time she only used the whistle after I'd embarrassed you so badly," Miku pointed out.

Conrad cleared his throat. "Yes. Good observation."

"Look," Raji began, getting heated once again, "even if I believe him, which I'm having a really hard time with, the Red Team is still too good. It's almost all eighth graders, and don't forget the ABCs!"

The students all looked at each other, but Raji was right. Even though Conrad was an outright *HyperBlast* star on his own, Annabella, Beverly, and Constance were fearsomely talented and easily better than Conrad as a squad. If they noticed Conrad's deception, they'd turn on him, and their vengeance would be swift and brutal.

"But we're not trying to win, Raji," Miku said, "we're trying to run out the clock, make the game last as long as possible, right, Eleanor?"

"Yes," Eleanor said. "I just need time to get in there. As much as you can give me."

"It just might work," Mr. Okafor said. "But you'll need my help, Eleanor. After all, if someone does see you, it's game over. At least I might give you some cover or a likely excuse for being there."

"Good idea," Eleanor said with a smile. "Thanks."

"Tomorrow it is, then," Miku said, standing up and placing her palms on the card table. "Second period, during our *HyperBlast* match, Eleanor and Mr. Okafor will infiltrate the library, and we'll give Coach Tasker a tournament for the ages!"

CHAPTER 11
THE DRAGON CAVES
OF PFAYLRIMOTH MOUNTAIN

THE MORNING'S SPRING shower turned into a downpour as Eleanor approached Brighton Middle. She pulled the hood up on her anorak raincoat, thankful for the excuse to shield her face from any possible onlookers. As she trudged up the great marble steps, one of the front double doors opened, revealing Mr. Okafor inside.

"Right on time," Mr. Okafor said, ushering Eleanor indoors. "The tournament has just started."

"Is it safe for me to come in?" Eleanor asked. "Will anyone see me?"

"It should be safe. Everyone's watching the match."

"Everyone?"

"Yes, today's the grand finale," Mr. Okafor explained. "The whole school participates, and all the students are either playing or waiting to play and watching on headsets along with most of the teachers, who are supervising. However, there are still a few teachers that we'll have to watch out for who could be *sympathetic* to Coach Tasker. Come with me."

Mr. Okafor led Eleanor through the silent hallways. The lights above were dimmed and flickering, as most of the building's electricity was being diverted to the tournament. Eleanor stealthily peeked through a door window and saw rows of students and the teacher in front plugged into their VR helmets. Apparently, individual student helmets had made a return appearance for the tournament, despite the school board's claim they'd been removed. This struck Eleanor as a serious oversight, given the charges of data theft.

Eleanor imagined Miku and the others were strapped into their simulators now, getting ready to wage battle. She hoped they'd be all right. With a little luck, she'd get the evidence she needed to shut down Coach Tasker's mysterious operation quickly and with as little trouble as possible.

Mr. Okafor stopped before the double doors of the school library. It was dark inside and looked like it was full of dust and cobwebs from sitting unused for months. Eleanor pulled on a door handle and found it locked.

"Allow me," Mr. Okafor said, pulling out a set of keys. "This is one of the perks of being an English teacher."

Mr. Okafor unlocked the doors and held them open briefly for Eleanor to enter. He checked over his shoulder briefly to make sure they hadn't been seen, and then entered the library himself.

"Eleanor," Mr. Okafor began once they were safely inside, "what happened in that phone call last night?"

"My producer, Barry, called me. I'd had him get a lab analysis of a sample of one of the SmartFüdz lunches."

"Oh, really?" Mr. Okafor replied. "What made you think to do that?"

"A hunch."

"And what were the results of the analysis?"

"I didn't want to tell the kids, but the lunch contained an experimental compound called . . . *Mesmerosin.*"

"I see," he said quietly. "And what does Mesmerosin do exactly?"

"Well, according to Barry, the compound affects the basal ganglia and the cerebellum, the parts of the brain that control the subconscious mind."

"What are you—"

"I think that's what Tasker and Peterson used to control Conrad," Eleanor replied. "And I think we're going to find the source of it in this library."

As Mr. Okafor opened the door and led them into the library, Eleanor thought back to that call. Barry had indeed confirmed Eleanor's suspicion about the presence of Mesmerosin; however, unfortunately, the scientists hadn't been able to tell Barry much else. It seemed as though the Mesmerosin was a very rare substance and not the type of thing most reputable laboratories spent time studying. However, one scientific journal showed that, in addition to the compound's noted effects on the brain, the brain itself seemed to affect the compound as well, like a rather twisted symbiotic relationship. According to the journals, it seems as though certain chemicals released by the brain, as a result of specific emotional responses—particularly kindness and compassion—were shown to *destabilize* Mesmerosin.

Eleanor thought back to the first time she encountered the Extractor at the factory, and Midrovia's agitation when she was patient and understanding during her mother's distressed phone call. And then she remembered Conrad and the way he'd reacted to overhearing Miku's touching story. As she walked into the library, she suddenly felt like all of the little clues she'd found were starting to add up and it gave her an idea. Of course, she'd have to explore it a little later and confirm if she was right, after she'd collected her evidence.

Even through the darkness, Eleanor could make out the sprawling layout of the library. The stacks were still lined with books, undisturbed since the day Principal Peterson dismissed physical books for learning. Mr. Okafor motioned for her to follow him. He led her to a winding staircase across the lobby, in front of a large, shuttered picture window, through which leaked the only natural light. She allowed herself a moment of jealousy: how fortunate these kids had been to have a grand library like this!

Then she peered over the railing to the library basement below. It was darker than the main hall, but Mr. Okafor was already descending the stairs, holding up his phone's flashlight to see. She felt a chill run down her spine, but she followed behind him.

The basement level was cluttered with boxes, which were lined up against a long hallway, and, at the end, there was a door. It had been left partially open, a crack really, and a bright green light emanated from within. Eleanor quietly rooted through her satchel for a moment, then pulled out her phone. She pushed the button on the side and returned it to her bag. Up ahead, Mr. Okafor was scanning his flashlight along the hallway walls, inspecting the boxes, and taking slow steps forward. Feeling prepared, Eleanor took a deep breath, squared her shoulders, and then charged ahead of him, not needing his light to see that this was the door she knew she wanted to open.

Eleanor reached for the handle to push it open and heard an electronic hum coming from inside the room. As she started to push the door open, and with a clever remark ready, she felt the piercing sting of a needle in her upper left arm. Then she lost consciousness.

....

Meanwhile, Miku, Tessa, and Raji sat strapped into their VR pods in the *HyperBlast* arena. They had all entered the staging area at least twenty minutes ago and were anxiously waiting for the start of the game, which had been mysteriously delayed. Miku looked across the blank expanse at the other players, who were growing increasingly impatient. The Newsers had ditched their usual camouflage avatars for new, intimidating spectacles. They were each a different mythical chimera: Tessa's avatar had the head of a lion with a dragon's tail, legs, and claws; Raji was buffalo-headed with an armored body like a rhinoceros; and Miku was a tiger with feathery wings and talons like a griffin. Conrad was formed as his usual, heroic Icarus avatar. He was huddled with the ABCs and occasionally shot withering stares over at Miku.

Earlier, they'd all agreed that Conrad must keep up his appearance as the cruel popular kid because any change in his attitude might draw suspicion from his Red Team team-mates, the ABCs, or, worse, Coach Tasker. His role in the plan was complicated because he needed to continue to play the skilled, confident *HyperBlast* champion, but not actually *win*. In many ways, this match would be the most difficult of all.

"Gamers! Prepare yourselves!" boomed Coach Tasker's voice from above them, and, as if in response to Miku's anxiety, she suddenly materialized in the blank sky above them. She floated in the air with one hand holding her bullhorn and the other clenched in a fist at her hip.

"The *HyperBlast* tournament will commence shortly," she announced curtly and vanished, but not before Miku caught sight of the red whistle hanging from her neck.

"You guys remember the plan?" Miku asked under her breath.

Tessa and Raji nodded.

"And you remember the map, right?" Miku asked.

"I should be asking you," Raji said. "I'm the one who suggested the map!"

In fact, Raji was responsible for the Blue Team's entire strategy. The layout of the game map was based on *The Dragon Caves of Pfaylrimoth Mountain*, the role-playing game Raji had discovered in his uncle's basement, and which the Newsers had spent many a Saturday night playing. For the first time in their middle school lives, Miku, Raji, and Tessa were more prepared than their opponents. They knew the shortcuts, escape routes, and bottlenecks, and they knew the best places to ambush the unsuspecting Red Team. They just hoped it was enough to buy Eleanor the time she needed.

"I just hope no one on the Red Team has ever played it," Tessa said.

"Are you kidding?" Raji asked sarcastically. "That'd be like saying that I have tried boxing."

"Yeah, Tessa," Miku agreed. "Of all the things that could go wrong today, that is probably the least of my concerns."

The Dragon Caves of Pfaylrimoth Mountain was decades old, and the Newsers were fairly sure it was discontinued. Even the game's country of origin was unclear because the rulebook was written in both Cyrillic and English. The game included a handful of many-sided dice and a detailed board that was a map of the titular mountain. Raji and the Newsers had committed the map to memory long ago through their many games, but then teaching all of the details of the layout to Conrad in one night so that he could recreate it within *HyperBlast* had been an interesting challenge. As reigning champion—and an unwitting pawn of Coach Tasker—Conrad always had the privilege of choosing the game maps for *HyperBlast*, but what Miku and the others didn't know until last night was that he was also able to design custom maps.

At the map's center was an expansive cavern floor known as the Dragon Pit. It was encircled by passages and smaller caves that had balconies and windows overlooking it. In a way it almost resembled a giant honeycomb or hive encasing a central gladiator-style arena that players could enter through the many pockets and openings in the rocks. The Red Team's flag would be down in the pit, while the Blue Team's would be high above in one of the many passages. Also hidden in the passages were stocks of extra HyperBalls for reloading.

If the Blue Team could secure the passageways early, they could hold their position indefinitely and force the Red Team to stay in the Dragon Pit to defend their flag. If everything went according to their plan, once the game began, Miku, Tessa, and Raji would lead small groups of Blue players through the passageways and into the caves and rain down offensive HyperBalls from higher ground. Then Conrad would consolidate his Red Team in the cavern floor in a siege-like standoff to protect the flag.

Suddenly, the blank staging area that everyone had been waiting in began to shift and swirl. Around them the dark, rocky forms of the dragon caves started to come into focus, lit by torches that lined the walls inscribed with crude hieroglyphs and runes. Ancient stone pillars and columns grew, outlining the mysterious and dank dragon caves of Pfaylrimoth Mountain. A deep, pounding noise echoed around the arena, getting louder and louder as the game map finished materializing.

"What's that racket?" Miku yelled to Tessa and Raji.

"Narcoleptic Puppies!" Tessa said gleefully. "It's one of my favorite hard-core punk bands!"

"Why is it playing now?" Raji said, holding his ears, which was kind of meaningless, because his real-world hands couldn't touch his real-world ears.

"I had Conrad add a soundtrack," Tessa yelled back, "to help distract the Red Team. It's like a psych-out, to get in their heads!"

"But what about *our* heads?" Raji complained.

"Players!" commanded Tasker's voice, somehow even louder than Tessa's hard-core music. "*HyperBlast* to commence in three ... two ... one ... Begin!"

Without any hesitation the Newsers jumped into action as Miku bellowed, "Blue Team, follow us if you want to win!"

....

Back in the library, Eleanor came to in a dark room, a corner of which was bathed in an eerie green light. She tried to look around, but found she could barely move her head, and the rest of her body was completely paralyzed. Panicked, Eleanor tried to yell but realized she was gagged.

"Our guest is awakening, Coach Tasker," Mr. Okafor said from somewhere behind Eleanor, sounding cold and machine-like, unlike the man she'd come to know.

"Excellent," came a familiar voice on the other side of the room.

Eleanor strained her eyes, looking as far to her right as she could to see on the periphery of her vision. In the darkness, she could make out a person removing a large VR helmet and getting up from a desk. The person who'd answered Mr. Okafor as Coach Tasker came into view.

No! Eleanor thought, as the realization struck her. *There was no "Coach Tasker." It was the strange man from the factory explosion, Gilmin Midrovia! He was playing as Tasker this whole time!*

Midrovia, still wearing his false nose and mustache, walked over to Eleanor and snapped his fingers in front of her face, watching her eyes flutter. Eleanor let out a garbled but unmistakable growl through the cloth tied around her mouth, which seemed to satisfy him. He then moved to the source of the green glow, a grow-light illuminating a glass tank filled with a moldy fungus. A *smelly*, moldy fungus just like the one at the SmartFüdz factory.

Eleanor recognized it at once and felt her heart start to race. It was the Mesmerosin Extractor.

"I'm very impressed, Eleanor Amplified," Midrovia taunted. "I don't know how you found me in a public middle school of all places. But found me you have."

Eleanor grumbled again, and Midrovia walked back to her and removed the gag.

"You know, calling for help is useless," he said. "No one can hear you down here."

"What if I just call you a deranged lunatic?" Eleanor replied.

"Equally useless!" Midrovia answered with a laugh.

"You won't be paralyzed for long, Eleanor," Mr. Okafor said, moving into her field of view. "You've only been given a small dose of the Mesmerosin, just enough to control your movement."

"Yes," Midrovia added gleefully. "Adisa here would know, since he gets much higher quantities and much more frequently. He and Principal Peterson took to the treatments quite successfully, unlike your little friend Conrad."

He knows about Conrad, Eleanor thought in a panic. *Miku and the others are in danger!*

"I-I don't know what you're—" Eleanor stammered.

"Of course, you do!" Midrovia snapped.

"I told him everything, Eleanor," Mr. Okafor said. "He knows Conrad is helping you and Miku."

"And now I have no choice," Midrovia said with a dramatic wave of his hands. "I must end my experiment, but at least I've gotten the results I need."

"What experiment?" Eleanor asked bitterly, hoping she could keep Midrovia talking long enough for her to come up with a plan.

"Why, this entire school, Ms. Amplified!" Midrovia explained. "Everything, from the virtual reality simulations, to the ZipTabs, the lunchroom food . . . it's all been engineered to advance my research into mind control!"

"What? W-what about Principal Peterson stealing kids' personal data?"

"Peterson was a rube! A patsy! A pawn!" Midrovia said, again gesturing wildly. "I was controlling him the whole time and made it appear he was stealing information. It was *me* taking the children's data for my research!"

"Then why use Conrad? Why a *student*?" Eleanor asked, exasperated.

"I had to! The Mesmerosin is so much more effective when subjects experience negative emotions like fear and especially jealousy. Ooh, yes, that's a good one."

"Conrad used the school's social boards to spread negativity, essentially manufacturing a culture of cruelty and division," Mr. Okafor explained automatically. "It was quite impressive, but it was something that only another student could truly accomplish."

"A student that all the others idolized and feared," Midrovia continued. "He's like my Trojan Horse of malevolence! At least, he *was*."

Midrovia walked back to the Mesmerosin tank and tapped on the glass. A little air bubble burbled from the fungus. He inspected it a moment, read a gauge fixed to the top of the tank, and twisted a nozzle gently, venting some of the gas in the tank into the air. He bent down and examined the fungus further.

"It's quite a fickle substance," Midrovia said. "I wish I could publish a book about it, but then I'd be thrown in prison, or worse!"

"Yeah? What's so special about it?" Eleanor asked, baiting him to reveal more. "All you managed to do was control a couple middle school staffers and a twelve-year-old."

Midrovia turned and glared at Eleanor before taking a breath and composing himself. "Of course, someone like you would never understand its true potential," Midrovia said. "Its effects vary greatly, depending on dosage. Use a lot at once and even a grown adult will listen to anything that I say."

While Midrovia continued to blabber on, Eleanor stared intently at Mr. Okafor and could swear that she saw the muscles in his face move ever so slightly.

"Unfortunately, that amount of control for an adult requires too much of the substance and constant reapplication, which, I'm sure you can understand, isn't very practical," Midrovia continued. "And even that is *unstable*, as the kid recently proved when he was able to break free of the chemical's grasp!"

Midrovia paused a moment and stroked his chin, considering the implications, before seemingly dismissing the thought.

Why he would so readily admit to the details of his nefarious scheme, Eleanor couldn't say. Like many of the villains Eleanor encountered, she guessed that his ego was so fragile, he just couldn't pass up the opportunity to brag.

"But I am a scientist, Ms. Amplified," Midrovia continued, "and not one to admit defeat. I've been testing various combinations of therapies on the adults and these students for months: subliminal suggestion, electromagnetic pulses, social conditioning.

"However, it wasn't until recently that I introduced trace amounts of Mesmerosin to the entire population; but now I believe I've developed the correct course of treatment to accomplish my goals."

"So, that's why you developed the lunch program," Eleanor said, putting the pieces together, "to sneak Mesmerosin into everyone's food. But what's that supposed to accomplish?"

"He's going to brainwash the school, Eleanor," Mr. Okafor said simply. "During the *HyperBlast* match."

"And you as well, Eleanor Amplified," Midrovia added with a cruel and wicked cackle.

CHAPTER 12

LEARN TO THINK, THINK TO LIVE

MIKU HELD HER HyperBlaster steady, crouched, and fired. Her HyperBall smashed into a Red Team member and then ricocheted away off the stone walls. Springing up, she grabbed another ball off the ground and reloaded as the pounding rhythms of Tessa's favorite punk bands banged on, all around them.

"Follow me!" Miku yelled, and motioned with her avatar's mighty paw for her small team to advance.

The match so far had been in the Blue Team's favor: they were easily holding the Red Team at bay and keeping them pinned in the central cavern, the Dragon Pit. Miku led her group of avatars through the caverns, intermittently pausing to look out from the balconies over the Red Team and pelt them with HyperBalls. As she ran down a corridor, she saw Raji approaching from the opposite direction.

"Raji!" she yelled. "What's your status?"

"We've kept the Reds contained on the eastern border," he replied, out of breath.

"Where's Tessa?"

"I just saw her; she's still active."

"Good. I hope we're giving Eleanor enough time."

"Me too," Raji said, "but I don't know how much longer we can keep this up."

Miku took her team to the edge of a cliff and surveyed the scene below. The Red Team was thrown off by their weak position and, for once, not being able to dominate the map. However, even with their sizable field advantage, the Blues wouldn't be able to hold the Red Team off forever.

Miku caught sight of Conrad's winged avatar. He was furiously directing his team, dodging balls, and periodically firing his HyperBlaster. He wasn't connecting with any Blue players, but was putting on a convincing show. Miku also saw the ABCs aggressively attacking the perimeter of the pit, their elven warriors a blur of athletic skill and prowess. For now, they were being held back by Blue Team members, but Miku knew it was only a matter of time before they broke through, stormed the upper chambers for the blue flag, and ended the game.

....

Meanwhile, a mind-controlled Mr. Okafor carried Eleanor through the empty hallways toward the gymnasium.

"Adisa, snap out of it!" Eleanor said angrily. "We can't let Midrovia get away with this!"

"The Professor is a great man," Mr. Okafor responded grimly. He didn't quite sound like he believed his words, but he continued nonetheless. "He has perfected his technique. Using a combination of prolonged electromagnetic exposure in the VR environment plus the Mesmerosin that the students, and you, have ingested, he'll be able to establish mind control *permanently.*"

"Wait. 'The Professor'?" Eleanor asked.

"You know him as Gilmin Midrovia."

Eleanor made a mental note about this clue to Midrovia's identity and decided to keep pressing to try to get as much information as she could before it was too late. She was thankful for one thing: her satchel was still slung around her torso and her phone was still inside, recording.

"So, this quote-unquote 'VR environment'—you mean the *HyperBlast* tournament, don't you? He's planning on exposing all the students playing and watching the game to these electromagnetic pulses?"

"Correct," Mr. Okafor said.

"And since Midrovia knew our plans," Eleanor continued with a growing sense of dread, "Miku and the others are all just sitting ducks."

"Also, correct," Mr. Okafor said, his voice strained slightly as he maneuvered and opened the gymnasium door with his foot. Eleanor thought it could be the sound of him fighting against the effects of the Mesmerosin.

"Adisa, you don't have to do this."

"Unfortunately, I do," he replied, then turned sideways to carry Eleanor into the gym. Inside were rows upon rows of students plugged into their VR pods, thrashing wildly as they battled inside the game.

Mr. Okafor carried Eleanor to the back of the arena, where there were two unused pods. He propped her up into the harness and buckled her in—for safety, after all—and gently lowered the VR helmet over Eleanor's head.

....

Miku was in the thick of battle, defending a key entryway to the caves against the relentless ABCs. HyperBalls bounded off the rocky walls all around her as she swung her HyperBlaster like a baseball bat, fending off enemy attacks. Beyond the enemy line, in the central area of the Dragon Pit, Miku saw two new players materialize onto the field. She squinted and could just make out the gray, frizzy-haired form of Ms. Brown's avatar standing next to Mr. Okafor.

"Eleanor! Mr. Okafor! What're you doing here?" she yelled, but it was no use. Miku was too far away from them, and the sound of students yelling and Tessa's music drowned her out.

That can't be a good sign, Miku thought before dodging a flurry of HyperBalls, and then looked around again. She hadn't seen Coach Tasker since the game began, but she knew she could materialize at any moment and was almost certainly still monitoring the game. If she somehow caught Eleanor and Mr. Okafor just standing there, they'd be done for.

"Raji!" Miku called over her shoulder. "Cover me! I'm going into the pit!"

"Miku, that's certain doom!" Raji shouted back, but he turned and fired his HyperBlaster into the opening, briefly clearing a path.

Miku charged through the hole he created, juking and swerving through the HyperBall fire. Mr. Okafor and Eleanor were now in the center of the cavern, in an open space next to the Red Team's flag. Miku checked and she was the only Blue Team member in the pit; the others were under orders not to go after the flag until either she, Raji, or Tessa gave the signal. She ran a few more paces, then dove at a nearby boulder, rolling her tiger-chimera body behind it. She peeked around the boulder and saw Mr. Okafor and Eleanor still standing there, not moving despite the raucous commotion and flying balls all around them. *That's odd*, she thought. *What're they waiting for?*

Suddenly a flurry of feathers landed in front of her. Miku stifled a surprised squeak and motioned for Conrad to quickly hide behind the boulder with her. He sharply whispered that he'd seen her enter the Dragon Pit, which was very much against the strategy they'd decided upon the night before.

"What're you doing here?" he asked anxiously, keeping his avatar and his voice low.

"Eleanor and Mr. Okafor are here!" she said quietly, pointing with her paw.

"Oh no. Do you think something went wrong?"

"I need to get to her," Miku said.

"Okay, I've got an idea," Conrad said, standing up. "Quickly, get in front of me."

Miku stood as Conrad flared his wings, then he wrapped her up under one, and running in unison, they charged across the field of battle. It looked a little awkward, but it was enough to shield Miku from any stray balls and hide her from the Red Team members for a moment. Together, they crossed the open expanse of the Dragon Pit and stopped in the middle, directly adjacent to the red flag, Eleanor, and Mr. Okafor.

"Hello, Miku," Mr. Okafor said placidly.

"Mr. Okafor! Eleanor!" Miku said breathlessly, peeking out from between some of Conrad's feathers. "What's wrong? Why're you—"

"Miku, listen to me," Eleanor blurted. "You've got to get out of here, get out of the game! It's Midrovia, he's planning on—"

"It's too late for that," Mr. Okafor interrupted, waving a hand to shush Eleanor. "The VR pods are locked, and we are staying put."

"Blast it, Adisa!" Eleanor yelled.

"Mr. Okafor? Why do you sound like that?" Miku said, concerned but also now a little afraid.

"His mind is being controlled, too!" Eleanor said, pushing away Mr. Okafor's hand and trying to reach Miku. "It's the Mesmerosin, Miku! That stuff I saw at the SmartFüdz factory; it's been in your school lunches, and it makes people susceptible to *mind control*! And any minute, Midrovia's going to—"

This time a deep rumbling sound cut off Eleanor, and it was deeper and more ominous than even Tessa's hard-core punk music. The cavern shook; dirt and rocks fell from the cave walls and ceiling as, suddenly, a great crack appeared before them, splitting the ground. The rumbling continued as fire and lava frothed out of the crack, widening and expanding before them as two winged claws reached out from the chasm and lugged behind them a massive, reptilian body.

"Take cover!" Miku yelled as the actual dragon of Pfaylrimoth Mountain lumbered forth out of the fiery crevasse.

The dragon snarled, swinging its snout back and forth, sniffing at all the avatar combatants scurrying around its cave.

A curl of smoke escaped its jaws as it beat its leathery wings and began to hover over the playing field. Around its neck, on a lanyard made of iron links, was a large, red whistle.

"It's Midrovia!" Eleanor yelled. "I mean Coach Tasker; they're the same—"

"Watch out!" Miku said as she leaped at Eleanor and dragged her to the ground, saving her from some falling debris.

"He's certainly got a flair for the dramatic," Mr. Okafor said calmly, hands clasped behind his back as chaos erupted around him.

The game ground to a halt as players looked out from the holes and openings surrounding the pit, glancing back and forth from the floor of the arena to the giant dragon, jaws slack in surprise. All the avatars' attention, as well as those watching from VR headsets sitting in classrooms, was focused squarely on this frightening beast.

"Children!" roared the dragon. "It's time for your final lesson ... in obedience!"

The dragon awkwardly reached for the red whistle around its neck with one of its winged claws while struggling to keep airborne as it flapped with one wing. As the Tasker dragon raised its whistle to its fiery jaws, Miku realized in horror that the dragon was just a spectacle to hold everyone's attention while Midrovia initiated his final feat of mind control.

"Miku!" Eleanor yelled. "You've only got one chance. The whistle works with the Mesmerosin in everyone's bodies, but you've never ingested it, so you could be immune! And it breaks down in the presence of—"

Eleanor's final word was drowned out by the pulsating frequencies emanating from the red whistle. The air in the cavern shook as the dragon flapped and blew the whistle, spraying shock waves of electromagnetic pulses instead of fire. Immediately, player avatars dropped their HyperBlasters and began to go limp, arms hanging at their sides. Raji's and Tessa's chimeras, who'd just been defending the outer caves, went still, as did Annabella's, Beverly's, and Constance's elven warriors; all of them stood dull and lifeless before the hypnotic signal. Eleanor, too, was caught in its grip as the signal interacted with the Mesmerosin in her system. Mr. Okafor looked no less placid than he had moments before, a look of contentment on his face.

Only Miku and Conrad were still mobile, though Conrad was uneasy on his feet and seemed to be battling the lingering effects of the Mesmerosin that had once been controlling him. Miku held on to his arm as he slowly bent over, grabbing his head and then his ears as he tried to block out the signal. He pitched forward onto his knees and looked at her. Unable to speak, he reached over, picked a HyperBall off the ground nearby, and threw it at the ground by her feet. Miku watched the ball bounce off the ground in front of her and, realizing his plan, fired her HyperBlaster away from him, into the air. They were now both defenseless.

"I declare a BlastOff with Conrad!" Miku hollered with all the gusto she could muster.

The dragon, which had been flapping and whistling the sinister signal above the field of play, froze in midair. The action and gameplay seized up and froze like a puddle in winter. The rumbling and shaking ceased; chunks of rocks and debris hung suspended. The player avatars evaporated, as did the Coach Tasker dragon, and then reappeared inside a Bundt cake–shaped force field, the dragon now replaced with the original avatar of Coach Tasker. In the center of the force field stood Miku and Conrad. Conrad was doubled over, the strain of resisting the mind-control rays still evident on his face.

Inside the force field, the other players still stood motionless and entranced while Coach Tasker, that is, Gilmin Midrovia, stalked back and forth, angry that his mind-control plot had been paused by a petulant twelve-year-old. Miku watched Coach Tasker and then looked back at Conrad and the others and she knew what was *really* at stake—they were stuck in this game, unable to leave until someone was declared a winner. Depending on the outcome, they would either be safe or they would be mind-controlled puppets. However, the game wouldn't continue until either Miku or Conrad ended the BlastOff, so it seemed, for the moment, that they were at an impasse.

Miku saw Eleanor's Ms. Brown avatar standing on the opposite side of the circle from Tasker. She ran over to her, banging on the force field, trying to get her attention, but Eleanor only blinked and stared back at Miku with a blank expression.

"It's no good!" Conrad said, holding his head.

"Well, what am I supposed to do?" Miku asked desperately.

"I don't know, but you've got to break the—" was all Conrad managed to say before collapsing on the ground.

Now, Miku was alone.

She looked around, and the only other person moving was Coach Tasker, or rather, the mysterious villain Gilmin Midrovia.

"Come now, girl," Midrovia yelled in his Coach Tasker avatar from behind the force field. "There's no escape here. Your friends are all under my control, as is your *hero*, Eleanor Amplified. I'm not going to hurt you. I only want you to join your friends and partake in the treatment. I'll erase these terrible memories and be on my way—you'll never have to think about me again!"

Miku turned away from him and looked at the emotionless faces of Tessa and Raji, her best friends and fellow reporters. If she had listened to them and not dug deeper into the problems with Principal Peterson or Conrad and the whole school—if she could have just been happy with their friendship and the newspaper—then maybe they wouldn't be in this mess. All they ever did was have her back and support her, and now look where they were. Then she found Eleanor and Mr. Okafor in the crowd, both looking pleasantly into the distance. Her throat burned as she thought of how kind and supportive Mr. Okafor was when she first came to him with the idea of starting *The Beacon*. He had always been there for her: to give her advice, to read her stories, to point her in the right direction, but now all of that was gone. And Eleanor! Miku had listened to *The Whole Story* every day after school when she first moved here, and she wanted nothing more than to be as clever and capable as Eleanor was. She was only at Brighton because of Miku. She had wanted to help make the city safer like Eleanor did, but all she managed to do was put everyone in more danger.

Then, she looked around at her classmates, most of whom had teased or scorned her for the better part of the school year.

While she couldn't honestly feel sympathy for all of them, she did know that none of them woke up this morning and expected to be frozen in the middle of a dragon pit because their middle school coach was trying to hypnotize them.

"Look, Miku," Midrovia said in a friendlier voice. "I've been watching you and your friends this whole time, and I have to give it to you—you were closer than anyone to figuring out my plans."

Finally, she looked back to Conrad, who was still unconscious. *Oh, Conrad,* Miku thought.

"I had no idea how tenacious you were, but you've really proven yourself as an ace reporter," Midrovia continued. "If you want, I can help you set everything right. Everyone will know the truth about Principal Peterson and the corruption here, and you'll be the one to tell the story—not Eleanor."

The last year had been miserable, and her heart had been completely broken because of Conrad. She remembered all the times that he had mocked her or posted mean comments or GIFs of her on the boards. How he had helped turn the whole school against itself and acted like he had never once been her best friend. Miku felt some dampness on her cheeks, but when she rubbed her paw over her face there was nothing there.

"I could help you, Miku," Midrovia said. "Call off the BlastOff and I'll help you fix everything. If you join me, we can make everything go back to *normal*."

Miku paused and felt her heart start to race. *Normal?* She looked around the Dragon Pit, at everyone frozen there, and the HyperBall that Conrad had thrown at her feet. *What would Midrovia know about making things go back to normal*, Miku thought. All of the changes, the VR, the ZipTabs, all happened *because* of him. The last year had happened because everyone had been under the influence of the cruel plots and experiments of Midrovia. The thought made her angry, and it was a salve on some of the sadness and guilt that she had been feeling only moments ago. This wasn't her fault; it was Midrovia's.

Miku straightened up and felt her anger quickly cool and harden into a steely resolve.

"Everyone!" Miku yelled as she began pacing around the interior of the force field, trying to meet the vacant gazes of her fellow students. "Last year, I was new to Brighton. I was nervous and scared and I didn't know anyone. But I had a feeling, even on the very first day," she said, looking down at Conrad and then up at Tessa and Raji, "that I'd meet lifelong friends here, and I wasn't disappointed!"

On the sidelines, the Coach Tasker avatar glared at Miku, clearly unhappy with the recent turn of events and that Miku wasn't currently getting her memories erased.

"With two of those friends, I started *The Brighton Beacon* newspaper, because I loved this school, and I wanted to be a part of its community—a community of curious, interesting kids. I made *The Beacon* to be a forum and a place for all of us to learn about each other and find out what was going on so we could all participate in that community!

"And then things changed. We stopped talking to each other, and instead we just believed everything we read or saw online. We didn't have facts, we had memes. We didn't talk, we gossiped. Our community wasn't working, because it was fractured and no one listened to each other. We started relying on virtual reality instead of real reality! And as a smart person recently told me," Miku said, taking a moment to breathe as she looked at Eleanor, "without common ground and a shared set of facts, a community can't work.

"But what I didn't know was that all this time we were being *manipulated*. All of us. By this guy!"

Miku said this last part quite dramatically and pointed an accusing finger at Coach Tasker.

"I mean, this lady . . . who's really just an avatar being controlled by a mad scientist guy. I haven't actually seen him— or Coach Tasker, for that matter—in real life, but that's my whole point! With the help of Eleanor Amplified, I know that Tasker's real name is Gilmin Midrovia, and he's a *villain*.

"He used Principal Peterson, and Conrad Praeder, and even Mr. Okafor to mess with us and to control us. He used them to spread confusion on the ZipTabs, made us fight each other in *HyperBlast*, and even put chemicals in our food! And now this dastardly fiend wants to tell us what to think, steal our memories, and probably worse, but we can't let him!"

Miku paused to catch her breath and her voice seemed to hang in the air across the entire virtual playing field. She looked at them all and willed her words to reach the silent students. But if they could hear her, they weren't showing it. Their avatars stood motionless, still apparently under the thrall of Midrovia's hypnotic whistle. Miku hung her head and sighed, trying to quickly think of what else she could say to help break Midrovia's control over everyone.

Then she noticed a slight movement out of the corner of her eye—something on the ground. She looked over and saw that Conrad's hand was twitching. Miku hurried to him and knelt, putting a hand on his back.

"Conrad?"

"Keep going, Miku," Conrad whispered.

Miku nodded, tightening her hand into a fist, and stood back up. She couldn't give up now; everyone needed her.

"Michelle Collette!" Miku said, pointing at a large troll avatar. "You're a natural leader and one of the best strategists I've ever seen. Think what would happen if you and the ABCs— the school's best athletes—teamed up? You'd be *unstoppable*."

Miku watched as the troll avatar started to wobble a little on her feet.

"And Ziara Ahmeed!" Miku said, turning and pointing at a cyborg-like avatar. "You're the best artist in the school, and your posts can be really funny. Raji Chandrasekhar is a hilarious writer. What if you worked with him, instead of insulting him? You two could create an amazing comic or something together!

"We all have so much in common," Miku said passionately as she turned to look at as many avatars as possible. "And I know we all have something that makes us each special. We each bring something to the school, be it Tessa Wilkins's social justice rallies, or Mr. Funches's chicken patty sandwiches. We all make Brighton what it is, and it lets us each bring something of ourselves to it. So let's fight for this school. Like it says right above the front doors, 'Learn to Think, Think to Live.' Let's think for ourselves and live our own lives without this weirdo trying to interfere in *our community!*"

Then Miku felt a hand on her shoulder. She looked over and saw Conrad smiling, and she couldn't stop the grin that appeared. Miku started to say something when he nodded toward the other students. When she turned back, she watched as the other students' avatars behind the force field, one by one, began returning to life. A gremlin shook his head with a confused look; two Viking warlords blinked and laughed and then hugged when they saw each other; a sphinx roared a great cheer; and it was quickly taken up by the rest of the players, all grateful to Miku for breaking the hypnotic spell.

However, there were two avatars who were not cheering. Eleanor and Mr. Okafor jumped and waved their hands on the other side of the force field. Miku, puzzled and a little embarrassed by the attention, waved. When Eleanor started waving even more frantically, Miku gestured with her hands and mouthed the word *What?*. Then Eleanor repeatedly pointed at something behind Miku at the other end of the force field. Or, in this case, a serious *nothing*, because the Coach Tasker avatar had disappeared.

"Conrad!" Miku said, grabbing his shoulder to get his attention. "Tasker's gone!"

"Hurry, we've got to end the game. Here!" Conrad said, tossing his ball up in the air toward Miku. "And don't forget to grab the red flag."

Miku smiled and caught the ball, which meant that Conrad was out and the BlastOff was over; however, the real game still had to be finished. As the force field melted away, the original gameplay was restored, debris continued to fall from the sky, active players were returned to their original positions, and eliminated players were moved to the waiting area. However, none of the players—Blue or Red—were interested in the game anymore.

From all around the arena, avatars began to swarm Miku in celebration and gratitude for releasing them from the dragon's hypnosis. "Mi-ku! Mi-ku! Mi-ku!" they chanted, and crowded around her avatar, effectively blocking her from getting to the Red Team's flag. No one could hear her protests as she tried to push through the crowd, and she looked around wildly for help. Finally, she spotted Tessa and Raji and locked eyes. Miku waved her hands over the heads of the other avatars and pointed emphatically at the flag while a small group tried to lift her up. Her friends looked from her to the unguarded flag and signaled that they understood—Tessa nodded and Raji gave a wink and two thumbs up—before they quickly made their way around the edge of the crowd to the flag.

At the top of a small mound were the flagpole and the cheerfully flapping red flag. Tessa and Raji glanced around to make sure no one was looking at them or was getting ready to launch a surprise attack. Watching them through the sea of avatars, Miku wanted to yell "Hurry it up" because it was clear to her that no one was even paying the slightest bit of attention to them. Then Tessa knelt and put her avatar paws on her knee while Raji climbed onto her back, as Tessa started to hoist him up. Miku held her breath as Raji stretched and reached for the flag. He missed once, and then firmly grabbed the flag with his claws and pulled it down as a buzzer sounded.

The Blue Team had *finally* won a match.

Out in the gymnasium, the safety releases on the VR pods disengaged and students began to pull off their helmets and unlock their harnesses. The room was full of chatter and excitement as all around the gym students were slowly emerging from their pods, a look of celebration on their faces. Miku ripped off her helmet and pried herself loose from the contraption. Next to her, Raji and Tessa were doing the same.

"Come on, you guys," Miku said, "we've got to find Eleanor."

The Newsers tore out of their VR pods in record time and navigated through the maze of metal and wires that made up the gymnasium. The lights were on for the first time that year and displayed the ugly latticework of machinery that helped suspend the game pods. Far up on the walls, behind thick, vinelike cables and wires, Miku saw the old banners from years past when Brighton still played basketball and volleyball. The Newsers broke through the double doors just as, down the hall, Eleanor and Mr. Okafor emerged from the gym's rear exit. Raji and Tessa cheered and whooped as Eleanor and Miku ran to each other and hugged.

"I'm proud of you, kid," Eleanor said.

Miku looked up at Eleanor and then hugged her tighter, hiding the tears of relief and happiness. Then Miku felt a gentle hand on her shoulder.

"Miku, I'm so sorry," Mr. Okafor said, looking at both of them, "and to you as well, Eleanor."

Miku and Eleanor finished their hug, and Eleanor stood, putting a hand on Mr. Okafor's arm.

"It's okay, Adisa. It wasn't your fault," Eleanor said, then squared her shoulders and looked at each of them in turn. "But now we've got to stop Midrovia!"

"I'm helping, too!" Conrad said, emerging from the double doors where Miku and the others had come from.

Miku was ecstatic to see Conrad for several reasons, but she especially wanted to celebrate their victory and a good plan, well executed. She started to run over to give him a hug when a piercing alarm sounded. Then fluorescent hallway lights cut off and pulsing emergency LEDs came on, highlighting the paths to the nearest exits. A second later, the sprinkler system engaged, soaking them.

"This is Midrovia's doing!" Eleanor yelled, covering her ears with the others to block out the alarm. "He's using this as a distraction while he gets away!"

"Children, please come with me; we've got to get outside!" Mr. Okafor yelled.

"What about Tasker?" Miku yelled back. "Or Gilmin Midrovia—whoever! We've got to help Eleanor!"

"No, Miku, go with Adisa!" Eleanor said sternly. "I'll find you afterward. I'm going alone this time."

Miku began to protest, but Tessa quickly tapped her shoulder and then shook her head. Raji and Conrad had already started for the exit and beckoned her to follow. Miku watched as Eleanor drew her raincoat around her and pulled the hood over her head. She looked at Miku and smiled, giving her a slight wave.

Then Eleanor turned and ran down the darkened hallway, heading for the library.

CHAPTER 13

THE WHOLE STORY

ELEANOR CHARGED DOWN the hallway, heading back to the dank library basement where she'd last seen the fiendish Gilmin Midrovia. The creepy "Professor," as Mr. Okafor had referred to him before, hadn't managed to brainwash the school, but that didn't make him any less dangerous. He could still take his technology elsewhere and try again unless she could stop him here and now.

At least Eleanor had figured out the weakness in Midrovia's mind-control technique, so she had that going for her, too. It matched up with what Barry had told her about the scientists' evaluation of Mesmerosin: it was destabilized by positive emotions in the brain. Specifically, Eleanor had deduced, by feelings of empathy, friendship, or love. First, the Mesmerosin had reacted in the SmartFüdz factory when she was talking with her distressed mother; it happened again with Conrad outside *The Beacon* office door; and then again with Miku's stirring speech to her fellow students.

Now she also understood why Midrovia had used Conrad to spread negativity and fear among the student population. If empathy and positivity would weaken Mesmerosin, the inverse must be true as well. Of course, she still didn't know *why* he'd done any of it, but she aimed to find out.

She slowed a little as she approached the double doors to the library, keeping an eye out for any signs of trouble. One door was left slightly ajar and she could smell smoke coming from inside. Had Midrovia been so heartless as to set fire to a middle school full of students? Eleanor shook her head at the thought, and was thankful that the alarm had sounded, ensuring the fire department was on its way. She checked the door handles for heat, but they were cool, so she pushed her way into the library.

Inside the library lobby, the emergency lights still blinked, giving the place an even creepier vibe than before. Next to a row of computers was a smoldering trash can, which Eleanor guessed was the source of the smoke that had triggered the fire alarm. She heard a noise and turned toward the picture window and basement stairwell. Coming up the stairs from his basement hideout was Gilmin Midrovia. The sprinklers had soaked him through, and he carried a duffle bag so stuffed that papers were sticking out every which way, and the Mesmerosin tank was nestled under his other arm.

"Hold it right there, villain!" Eleanor shouted. In retrospect, she wished she'd called him something worse than "villain," but she couldn't bring herself to use foul language in a school.

"Ah, Ms. Amplified!" Midrovia said, his voice taking on a panicked register. "We meet again. I'm afraid I can't talk right now, you understand. I've got a pressing engagement—"

"Why, Midrovia?" Eleanor demanded, in no mood for banter. "What kind of monster would put school kids in danger like this?"

"These children were never in any danger!" Midrovia declared indignantly. "I am an academic, madam, and my interests here were purely *scientific* in nature."

"That's about as believable as your fake nose."

Midrovia gasped and dropped his duffle bag, immediately touching his false nose and mustache to make sure they were still in place.

"How rude," he said. "But, *honestly*, I don't care if you believe me or not."

Midrovia moved a foot forward, testing to see if she would try to stop him. But Eleanor countered quickly, making it clear she wasn't about to let him leave that easily. He seemed to consider his options, but Eleanor knew that he'd have a hard time getting by her, especially with the bulky Mesmerosin Extractor. They were at a stalemate, for the moment at least.

"You've been well funded all this time," Eleanor said, nodding to Midrovia's bag and the Mesmerosin as the pieces of this particular puzzle started coming together. Then, with a small spark of hope, she thought about her phone in her satchel, which she realized she'd never turned off recording mode.

"*SmartFüdz, SuperInteliCom*, all this technology," Eleanor continued. "How does an everyday crook like you get those kinds of resources?"

"I told you I was conducting research, Eleanor Amplified. Let's just say there are motivated parties—benefactors, if you will—who are very interested in my results."

"Lots of money in brainwashing, huh?" Eleanor replied sarcastically.

"Like you wouldn't *believe*."

"So you're a lackey. A pawn working for someone else?" Eleanor said, trying to keep Midrovia talking. "And this someone has deep pockets and access to very sophisticated technology—it must be a pretty powerful entity. Or maybe it's several someones . . ."

"Okay, I think that's quite enough sleuthing for today!" Midrovia said, growing concerned. "Lars, *now!*"

From behind Eleanor came a thumping, lumbering sound, like a dump truck with a flat tire barreling toward her. Out of the shadows surged Midrovia's henchman: the humongous, trench-coated man Eleanor had last seen before the factory exploded. He held a photocopier over his head and lunged at Eleanor. Quickly, she ducked to the side and rolled just as Lars launched the copier over where she was standing and through the picture window, sending a spray of glass shards and wood onto the lawn below.

"Until next time, Eleanor Amplified!" Midrovia shrieked as he tossed the duffle bag through the gaping window. Then he pulled out a small test tube from the inner pocket in his lab coat and threw it into the still smoldering trash can. A bright blast erupted from the can, as Eleanor shielded her eyes, and a shower of sparks and plumes of smoke and ash rained down on the library's main hall. Eleanor coughed and called out Midrovia's name as she tried to find him in the haze.

When the smoke cleared, "Gilmin Midrovia" and his hench-man, Lars, were gone.

....

Eleanor sat back in her seat in her darkened studio, the red light above her providing just enough light to see her script and notes. She looked up and saw the clock counting down the final seconds of her sponsorship break, giving her a moment or two more before she went live again to her millions of listeners. She was glad to be back broadcasting the news, and particularly happy not to be a brainwashed drone—thanks to Miku—but she was still troubled.

"Five seconds, Eleanor," Barry said over the intercom.

"Got it."

"Four . . . three . . . two . . ."

There was silence, and then the subtle buzz in her headset as she heard her microphone turn back on, and the "ON AIR" light above her turned green.

"We're back with *The Whole Story*, listeners. I'm Eleanor Amplified," she began. "The Case of the Mind-Controlled Middle School is finally closed, thanks in no small part to the bravery of a young reporter and her friends.

"After the events that occurred a few weeks ago, Brighton Middle has returned to normal. All traces of the criminal experiments in mind control have been removed, and the principal, Marvin Peterson, was reinstated after being exonerated for his role in the scheme. The school board found that because of his brainwashing, he was as much a victim as the students. Parents, understandably, are furious. But the district has promised a full investigation into how this mysterious criminal was able to infiltrate the school in the first place.

"The plot involved a master criminal, a Gilmin Midrovia, and a henchman he called Lars—although I believe the names to be fake. Using shadow companies and state-of-the-art technology, Midrovia managed to turn Brighton Middle School into his own evil science experiment; and the students were his lab rats. With a mix of negative subliminal messages, electromagnetic signals, and a substance called Mesmerosin, Midrovia effectively developed a technique for mind control on Brighton's students and faculty.

"At first, I didn't see the extent of the plot. You might remember that, a few weeks ago, I dismissed the trouble at the school as simply a case of a corrupt school principal stealing student data. However, this case turned out to be much more than a violation of privacy, as one student, Miku Tangeroa, repeatedly tried to tell me—and she was right. It was a good reminder that getting to the truth can take a while, it's not always obvious, and sometimes you need help.

"So, the good news? Midrovia's vile experiment has been shut down, and Brighton's students are safe. The bad news: the criminal himself is still at large, and we are left with some unsettling questions. What is the true identity of the fiendish Gilmin Midrovia? When could he strike again? And perhaps most worrisome of all, who was financing his sophisticated criminal exploits? I'll stay on the case and report back here on *The Whole Story*. I'm Eleanor Amplified. Until next time, listeners!"

Eleanor's mic cut off, and she listened to her show's closing theme music over the studio monitors. She took off her headphones and rolled her head, stretching her neck.

Barry's voice came over the intercom. "Great show, Eleanor."

"Thanks, Barry."

"And you've got a visitor."

"Oh?"

Barely a second had passed when Miku suddenly bounded through the studio door, threw her arms around Eleanor, and squeezed.

"Hey, kid, leave me some room to breathe!" Eleanor said with a laugh. "I guess things are going well back at Brighton?"

"Everything's great! It feels like a regular school again. Raji and Tessa say 'hi,'" Miku said, and then slyly added, "So does Mr. Okafor."

Eleanor smiled and thought for a moment. "Well, please do send my best wishes. And how're you and Conrad?"

"Oh! We're, ah—" Miku stammered, turning red. "We're going on our first date, tomorrow after school."

"That's really great."

"Yeah, and *The Brighton Beacon* is running again!" Miku added, desperate to change the topic. "Tessa has started doing concert reviews, and Raji has got a new humor column with Ziara drawing cartoons. It's hysterical!"

"Amazing. I'd love to read it."

"I'll send you a copy. Oh, and—" Miku said, remembering the last update she wanted to share with Eleanor. "Ms. Brown got her job back! She's back teaching Social Studies. She said that judging by the students' quiz scores, her replacement must have been slightly better than mediocre!"

"What a compliment," Eleanor said laconically, although she secretly appreciated it.

Then Miku's face grew concerned. "Do you have any leads on Midrovia or his henchman?"

"No, but thanks to that trick you showed me," Eleanor said, pulling out her smartphone, "I got the evidence I needed to prove he was the one behind all of this, and to clear Principal Peterson and Adisa, er, Mr. Okafor. I gave all of it to the police. In fact, without those recordings, I think we'd be back at square one."

"But aren't we starting from scratch anyway?" Miku asked with a sigh. "We don't even know who Gilmin Midrovia is."

"It's true," Eleanor said, getting up from her desk. "But we know that Adisa called him 'the Professor,' and he referred to himself as an academic when I questioned him at the library. And he claimed to be doing research for a mysterious 'benefactor.' So, whoever he meant would have to have serious resources, like the millions-of-dollars kind."

"Wow," Miku said. "Like a supervillain."

Eleanor looked at her and began to pace around her tiny studio. "Maybe," she said. "Or perhaps supervillains—there could be more than one."

Then the door to the studio opened, and Barry and Mr. Richman walked in. Mr. Richman looked pensive, with a slight touch of concern, and Barry, as usual, had his head buried in papers.

"We've got a lot to record this afternoon, Eleanor," Barry said, in a way that Eleanor had learned meant he was thinking of how behind he'd gotten recently, thanks to his famous radio host being away from the studio and off fighting crime. "We'll probably have to work through the weekend in order to—"

"Eleanor," Mr. Richman interrupted, "I saw something in the newspaper this morning that got me thinking."

"Oh?" Eleanor replied, knowing that when Mr. Richman got to thinking, it usually meant she was about to be handed another dangerous assignment.

"I saw a story, buried deep in the back of the paper, a little local piece," Mr. Richman said. "It was about some administrators at Union City University. Apparently, some mid-level managers were in hot water over mishandling their budgets. The university claimed that graduate students were complaining about how they were working on bogus experiments and that inventory from the chemistry department had recently gone missing."

"I see," Eleanor said thoughtfully. "You think there could be a connection to—"

"There's one more thing," Richman said. "An *eyewitness* claims to have seen a man stealing heavy equipment out of a laboratory one night. Apparently, this man was—" Richman stopped and flipped to the right page in the newspaper, reading directly from the quoted passage "—'extraordinarily humongous.'"

"Well, then," Eleanor said, grabbing her satchel from the back of her chair. "It sounds like something I should probably investigate."

"Before you do, Eleanor," Miku said, reaching for her arm, "I never thanked you. For, well, for everything."

Eleanor smiled, waited a beat, and then said playfully, "Well, technically, you still haven't *thanked* me, you've only noted that you have yet to—"

"Thank you, Eleanor!" Miku said brightly. "For everything."

"You're welcome," Eleanor replied. "But I should be thanking *you* for all the hard work you put in to cracking this case. I couldn't have done it without you."

There was a moment of silence, and then Miku said, "You know, technically, you didn't thank me either, just now—"

"Thank you, Miku!" Eleanor said, laughing.

"You're going to make a great reporter someday, kid," Mr. Richman added.

"Actually, Chief," Eleanor said, "I think she's a pretty great reporter right now."

Across town, deep, deep underground, a maniacal laugh echoed through the sewers of Union City. A rat, scurrying through the damp caverns with a chicken wing in its jaws, paused and stood on its haunches, trying to locate the sound. Then, directly above the rat, a manhole cover shifted, letting in a shaft of light before a large, moose-sized man climbed in, pulled the cover back into place, and began lumbering down the metal rungs of the sewer ladder. The rat scampered away with a small squeak, still clutching the chicken wing, wanting nothing to do with the unwanted visitor. The man dropped into the dark sewer below and expertly began moving his hands along the concrete walls as the laughter continued to bounce off the walls around him.

Finally, he located a brick that was jutting out from its original position. He tugged on it, triggering a hidden doorway to open and exposing the source of the creepy, crazed-sounding laughter. The huge henchman stepped into the secret hideaway of Gilmin Midrovia and started to join in on the evil laughter as the hidden door began to slide shut.

"No, Lars," Midrovia cried, "evil laughter is for masterminds *only!*"

"Sorry, boss," Lars said in a sad deep baritone.

What evil scheme was Midrovia hatching? What malevolent plot was he concocting? Only time will tell, but, without any doubt, the next time this mysterious criminal decides to wreak havoc upon the good people of Union City, he and his henchman will have to contend with our hero, Eleanor Amplified.

ACKNOWLEDGMENTS

I WOULD LIKE to sincerely thank, first and foremost, you, the reader and possibly also podcast listener—really anyone who's let *Eleanor Amplified* live in their imagination for a bit. I am endlessly grateful. I am also grateful to lots and lots of people who've helped me make *Eleanor Amplified* over the years (first as a podcast, and now, hey, as a book), some of whom I will mention here: actors Christa D'Agostino, Elisabeth Kellner, Kevin Pfluger, Scott Johnston, and Jim Barton; WHYY leadership Kyra McGrath, Bill Marrazzo, and Gabriel Coan; (fantastic) editor Britny Brooks at Running Press; mentors and favorite persons ever Terry Gross and Danny Miller and everyone at *Fresh Air*. There really are many more people to thank, and I probably *should* mention them too, but doesn't almost everyone skip the Acknowledgments? I know I do. To the person reading this, are you a superfan (a serious *Eleanerd*) and not just someone mentioned above? I feel like if you are, there should be some kind of payoff to reading this. Right? Okay, here's an Easter egg: the character Gilmin Midrovia we just saw in the sewer in the final chapter is really the villainous Vladimir Ignomi from the podcast! It all ties together! You probably figured that out already. But now it's confirmed, just for you. Thank you, again.